Penguin Crime Fiction
Editor: Julian Symons
The Fun House

Philip Reid is the pseudonym for Andrew Osmond
and Richard Ingrams.

Philip Reid

The Fun House

Penguin Books Inc
New York · Baltimore

Penguin Books Inc
72 Fifth Avenue, New York, New York 10011

Penguin Books Inc
7110 Ambassador Road, Baltimore, Maryland 21207

Originally published in Great Britain under the title
    Harris in Wonderland by Jonathan Cape, 1973
First published in the United States by Houghton Mifflin
    Company, Boston, 1974
Published by Penguin Books Inc, 1976

Made and printed in Great Britain by
Hunt Barnard Printing Ltd, Aylesbury, Bucks
Set in Intertype Times

Contents

To release the truth against whatever odds, even if so doing can no longer help the Commonwealth, is a necessity for the soul.

HILAIRE BELLOC

1 The *Defendant*

I got back to London on the first Sunday in November. It wasn't until Wednesday that I felt sufficiently restored to pay a visit to the *Sunday Defendant*, and that was the day my troubles began. I should have stayed at home.

I had been in Cornwall trying to get my book on the Trans-Equatorial Mining Company into some kind of shape. It was a big book, as befitted one of the biggest mining companies in the world, and its object was to expose the way T.E.M.C. have bought up politicians to get themselves the best concessions. I was quite pleased with it. All I needed now was a publisher and someone to buy the serial rights, which was where the *Defendant* came in.

I have never been exactly *persona grata* with the *Defendant*. They print quite a lot of my stuff, usually in their colour supplement, where its effect is somewhat blunted by all those porno ads. Quite often, if they want to disassociate themselves, they will put 'By Stuart Harris – A Personal View' so that readers know the Editor doesn't go along with my cynical assessment of the issues of the day.

They also suspect me of giving stories about them to the *Maggot*. Which I do, sometimes. But I'm not the only one.

It was a damp dark day and most of the windows of the *Defendant*'s ugly glass slab were lit up although it was early afternoon. As usual, on passing through the automatic portals I was struck by a feeling of depression. The lobby was got up like an Aztec temple; one glance at that was enough to make one doubt the whole concept of the *Defendant*. As I crossed the marble floor the commissionaire stared at me suspiciously from his glass booth, yet I must have been in and out of there a hundred times.

To forestall any confrontation I strode straight past him and into the lift, and not feeling ready to face the Editor, got out at the second floor and called on the 'Background' offices. 'Background' do those mammoth 'in-depth' investigations which help to make the *Defendant* the most unreadable paper in Fleet Street.

Actually, that's a bit unfair. The 'Background' men have brains even if they can't write deathless prose. Also they will, if need be, devote months to uncovering some piece of complicated skulduggery which would be beyond the powers of most reporters. Sometimes I help them out, on a freelance basis of course. They were all at Oxford together and any outsider is made to feel *de trop*. But if the dig is a big one they allow a few amateurs like me on the site to help sift through the dirt.

Only Burgess was in the office when I called. He was sitting with his feet on his desk drinking whisky and reading *Kidnapped*.

'Harris, you bastard!'

He swung his feet off the desk and took out another glass.

Burgess is the head of the 'Background' team. After Oxford he went into the Treasury, but couldn't stand the lack of publicity and moved to the *Defendant*. He illustrates the classic dilemma of the journalist: he wants to influence events but could never face public office. Power is what matters to Burgess. He is always going on about the people who've been ruined by a 'Background' investigation – 'wasted' is his word for it. He is a tall, swashbuckling man with a lot of charm and no taste whatsoever. He wears outrageous floral shirts which he picks up cheap in the sales.

'Where have you been?' he asked.

'Cornwall. I've written a book on T.E.M.C.'

'You bastard!' He grinned raffishly and lit a panatella. It obviously wasn't his busy day.

'I've come to flog the serial rights,' I said.

Burgess chewed the end of his cigar like a bandit and started blowing smoke-rings. Sometimes I thought he only smoked at all to show off this trick. 'I presume the tone of this book is not exactly friendly?' he said. 'To the company, I mean.'

'Not exactly. Do you think Peacock might be interested?'

Peacock was the Editor.

Burgess pulled a face. 'He might. Depends on how well he's forgotten that piece in the *Maggot* about his expense account. He thinks you were the source.'

'Balls.'

'I quite agree. But you know what he's like.'

I did. I gulped down the whisky and felt I could now face Peacock. 'I'll be around if you want anything doing,' I said. 'Thanks for the drink.'

Peacock's office was on the next floor, complete with carpet and a secretary guarding the door, who asked me if I had an appointment.

'Er . . . no, actually.'

She spoke into the intercom, which barked back, 'Stuart Harris? All right, send him in.'

Peacock rose from behind his desk like a headmaster. He is an unimpressive little man with a barking voice and that hounded look which you see in the higher echelons of television and the press. Is it overwork or suspicion of their colleagues? I don't know, but the higher they rise the more neurotic they become. With Peacock was another man whom he introduced as the Editor of the *Business News*, then scrambled back behind his desk.

'Well, Harris, what can I do for you?'

I briefed him on the book and the mutual advantages that would accrue from its serialization in the *Defendant*.

To my surprise the other man put his oar in. In a casual voice he mentioned that the *Business News* had lined up a feature on T.E.M.C. and that the company were flying two reporters out to Zambia next week. Peacock gazed at him as though trying to decide whether he was real, then turned back to me. 'Look, Harris, leave it with my secretary and I'll give you a ring when I've had a chance to look it over. Have you got another copy?'

'Yes.'

In fact I was so scared of losing it I had lodged the manuscript in my bank.

'Good,' said Peacock. 'Well you hang on to that, and we'll let you have this back as soon as we can.'

I bowed out. On the way down I called in to cry on Burgess's shoulder.

'You ought to get an agent,' he said.

'Yes,' I said. People were always telling me that. 'By the way, I'm going to Amsterdam.'

'Really?'

'A well-deserved dirty weekend. Tell Peacock I'll be back next week if he wants to get in touch.'

Burgess was lighting another cigar, manipulating it with his teeth. 'Well enjoy yourself. Mind you don't get the clap.'

It was possible to like Burgess once you knew what a disgusting person he was.

2 Dinner with Bosie

I was due at the Bosanquets' place at six but because of the rush hour was nearly half an hour late. For me the worst of being poor is waiting in bus queues. But if that's the price of not working for Peacock, I'll pay it.

Some months before, when the cash position had been critical, I had answered a classified ad in *The Times* for a part-time tutor. To my surprise the advertiser turned out to be Walter Bosanquet, the Labour politician. Bosanquet had been Foreign Secretary in the last Labour Government and was now in Opposition. A campaign was growing to make him Leader of the Party, and if the pollsters' predictions were right it was on the cards that I was in the employ of a future Prime Minister. That is the sort of thought which helps in bus queues.

I myself have never taken much interest in British politics, preferring the drama of Africa and Asia to the shuffling compromises of the Palace of Westminster. But Bosanquet was a cut above the average front bencher. Before I took the job I looked him up in a popular vade-mecum. It said:

Despite his working-class background – his father was a steelworker – Bosanquet mixes easily in any society. A grammar-school boy who won a scholarship to Cambridge, he has always taken pleasure in the company of intellectuals, a fact that excites the suspicion of some of his more humdrum colleagues. His book on the Irish Civil War is widely held to be a minor classic . . .

The job was a cinch. Four hours a week at five guineas an hour, a useful boost to the Harris budget. Bosanquet, whether from principle or prudence I couldn't decide, had sent his son to the local comprehensive and now the boy needed cramming. He was thirteen and his name was Barry. We got on quite well. He was a bit like me, brainy but idle.

Mrs Bosanquet opened the door. She was wearing an apron, but still looked as good as a woman of fifty can look. She wrote romantic novels under a pen-name and came from a higher social stratum than her husband. I apologized for being late.

'Oh, never mind that. Stay for dinner if you like. Barry's upstairs with his beastly guitar. How's your book going?' She didn't wait to hear the answer, but took my coat and ran off to the kitchen. 'Do stay for dinner. We need an extra man. Something's burning, don't tell me . . . '

The Bosanquets lived in Holland Park, in a large house which was comfy but not luxurious. They had excellent taste. There were good antiques and pictures scattered about, and going upstairs I made my way past prints by Dufy and Matisse on the landing. The balance was nicely judged: elegance without opulence.

Yes, I thought, I'd stay for dinner. Bosanquet probably wouldn't turn up; he'd be at the House. I hadn't actually seen him since he hired me, but I thought we'd agree about most things. As far as politics allow he was a man of principle, a liberal basically, not too wedded to socialist dogma, which was more or less my own position.

Barry's room was at the top.

'Hi Prof,' he greeted me.

There must be hundreds of Barrys in this part of London, I thought; long-haired and spotty, their accents half-Cockney, half-posh, living in rooms like this with records and pin-ups and guitars. I noticed a copy of the *Maggot* by his bed.

'Hello numbskull,' I said.

We spent the next hour discussing the foreign policy of George III, each of us doing his best to disguise from the other his lack of interest in the subject. Then I suddenly remembered I'd arranged to meet Midgely. Midgely was a ledger clerk working in the London office of Dynatrax, the pharmaceutical company; a weasel-faced man who looked undernourished and consoled himself for failure with Marxist politics. On the lookout for cracks in the system, he had found something shady in the Dynatrax books and had sent me photocopies through the post. Needing further explanation I'd arranged to meet him in a pub in the city that evening.

'Damn,' I said.

Barry wagged a finger. 'You shouldn't swear.'

I looked blankly at him. 'No, I agreed to see this bloke about a story. Oh hell, I'm supposed to be having dinner with your parents.'

'Well tell him you can't make it. Go on, there's a phone in dad's study.'

He took me down a floor and into a large book-lined room. I looked around. Rows of orange Left Book Club editions suggested a radical past. The modern books were mostly about The Environment, population growth, pollution. There were photographs on the mantelpiece: Bosanquet with Bevan, Bosanquet in uniform with Churchill, Bosanquet with Bertrand Russell. Volumes of Hansard lay piled in one corner. Mrs Bosanquet was at the desk with paper and pencil working on a diagram which I later realized was a seating plan for dinner.

'Oh . . . sorry,' I said, backing out the door and getting a punch in the ribs from Barry.

But she jumped up and moved to another table. 'Don't mind me,' she said. 'Please carry on. Where on earth am I going to put Marjorie? All she can talk about is horses.'

Barry just stood there grinning.

Fumbling with embarrassment I looked up the number of the pub, telephoned Midgely and told him I couldn't make it. He was annoyed of course. Like all informers he was sure his story was the big one. But I told him I'd got the photostats with me and would call him when I got back from Amsterdam.

'Now,' said Mrs B, 'let's all have a drink,' and we went downstairs to the sitting-room, where she poured me an enormous gin and tonic. She appeared to be distracted but was nothing of the kind. Her vagueness was a well-drilled act designed to tell her guests three things: 'I am far too intelligent a woman to be doing these chores,' but 'We're socialists so can't have domestic servants,' therefore 'Things may go wrong but I don't care so you needn't either.' I was about to admire the Worcester mugs when the doorbell rang and she brought in a grey-haired man, too well-dressed to be heterosexual.

'Desmond, what are you drinking? Stuart, be a darling. Run to the kitchen and get some ice.'

When I got back the party had been strengthened by two new arrivals. I recognized Chesterton, editor of a popular daily, and his wife, reputed to be a bit of a nympho. Chesterton had been a success, boosting the sales of his paper to a million. I quite liked the look of his wife.

More people came. I retreated to a seat in a corner. None of them took any notice of me. Desmond O'Riordhan, the first arrival, was a publisher with a line in coffee-table books and there was some discussion of a lavish history of the Paris Commune which his firm had just brought out.

'You did it proud,' he said to Chesterton. 'Just for that, we've booked some more ads.'

Chesterton laughed, showing a rather dirty set of teeth, at odds with his otherwise sleek appearance. 'We endeavour to give satisfaction,' he said.

Mrs Bosanquet was talking gardens with his wife. Barry had vanished. I began to feel bored.

Two more guests arrived, a merchant banker and his pretty diamond-spattered wife. They all seemed to know each other.

Dinner was nicely judged. Casseroled pheasant with claret, decanted so we couldn't see the label, homely china and not too much silver. I found myself parked beside the lady whose only interest was the Turf. She chattered on in the candlelight about her recent successes, telling me of some new club which tipped winners using a computer, then suddenly, as such women do, switched subjects and asked me what I did.

I had just embarked on a commercial for my book when the merchant banker cut in from across the table: 'What's that about T.E.M.C.?'

It was said casually, but he was interested.

'I've just written a book about it.'

'I do so envy you,' squawked the lady punter. 'To be able to write a book. Do you use these?'

She was a chain-smoker and was now lighting up between courses. As she drew on the fag, the banker came back at me: 'Why Trans-Equatorial?'

'I'm interested,' I said. 'The way they operate in South America, for instance.'

'How do you mean?'

'Well I suppose it's a form of bribery, really. With politicians.'

The banker smiled, a polite Old-Etonian kind of smile. 'We all need friends in high places,' he said, glancing coyly at Mrs Bosanquet. A place had been laid in case her husband managed to get away from the debate. It was strange how that empty chair seemed to dominate the room.

'Walter says the next Labour Government will *have* to do something about the City,' she said loyally.

'Every Labour politician says that in Opposition,' replied the banker and turned back to me. 'I want to know why you're so interested in Trans-Equatorial. What are you going to say in this book of yours?'

I gave him a synopsis, and when the women left the table he continued the cross-examination in earnest. The other men joined the conversation, which began to resemble a tribunal. Desmond, the publisher, agreed reluctantly to read the book, so I told him to get in touch with Peacock, trying to create the impression that everyone in London was after it.

When I mentioned the *Defendant* the merchant banker got quite nasty, berating me with T.E.M.C.'s profit record and contribution to the balance of payments. To attack so successful a company, he implied, was an unpatriotic act.

16

The only one on my side was Chesterton. After two glasses of port he offered me a job, but I turned him down. I couldn't stand the look of those teeth.

3 A Nasty Surprise

The next day things began to go wrong; small things at first, in which no pattern was apparent.

First I lost my briefcase. I was in the bank collecting travellers' cheques and had parked it on the floor by my feet. It was lunchtime and a small queue of customers had started to form at each till. Conscious of people behind me I signed the cheques as quickly as I could while the clerk made an entry in my passport, and that must have been the moment I was robbed. A girl who had just joined the queue said the man behind me had given up waiting and walked out with a briefcase; naturally she thought it was his. We ran into the street to look for him, followed by a posse of bank clerks and customers. All the girl could remember was that he was wearing a mackintosh. Needless to say he got away, and the search was abandoned to the fuzz, who remarked superfluously that the streets were full of men in macs with briefcases.

I bought the girl a drink and went home to pack, feeling more annoyed than downcast. At least I had the cheques and my passport. On the debit side I'd lost some notes and correspondence, the morning papers and an essay of Barry's on Lord North which I was happy not to have to read. More serious was the loss of the Dynatrax documents, though that too was not disastrous, since they wouldn't mean much to a snatch-thief and Midgely could always make fresh copies.

The immediate question was whether to postpone my visit to Amsterdam. I decided against it, and flew off that evening. I had promised myself a holiday – a reward for finishing the book. With that in mind Amsterdam seemed a good place to go. People said it was the City of the Seventies. I hadn't been there before, and vaguely hoped to meet the girl of my dreams.

2

I suppose I enjoyed it. To be honest, I can't remember much about the place. Canals, quaint houses, Rembrandt, hippies, seagulls. It was colder than London. On Saturday I changed my hotel because someone had gone through my luggage, and that night an Irishman took me to a club called the English Disease where you can drink draught bitter and see what the butler missed. On Sunday I got drunk and spent the afternoon in a cinema. I didn't meet any girls. On Monday I ran out of guilders and decided to fly back that night.

I was waiting for the flight to be called when a man came up to me in the airport bar, narrowing his eyes and pointing at my face.

'I know you,' he said.

An American wearing an Afghan sheepskin.

'Oh ... do you?'

This sort of thing happens all the time to people who appear on television, though that can't explain it in my case, since owing to a slight impediment of speech or perhaps the lack of an agent I've never been on the box. I just have the sort of face which people think they've seen before. They rush up and grab me at parties or on railway stations, eyes blazing with excitement, and shout 'Philip!' or 'Max!' and get quite annoyed when I deny it. So I smiled at this American, to show that though I didn't know him from Adam I bore him no ill will.

He stared at me a moment longer, then struck the bar with the flat of his hand.

'Harris!' he cried.

'That's right,' I said.

'Hot damn, it's Harris!'

'I'm afraid I don't ...'

He made a dismissive gesture, as if to say he was the most forgettable person in the world, and held out his hand. 'Henry Arbuthnot. Oxford, fifty-nine. We used to play poker.'

'Really?'

'We must drink to this. What's yours?'

At that point the flight was announced and trying not to look relieved, I made my excuses. But Arbuthnot picked up his bags.

18

'You're going to London? Great. Let's grab a seat up front.'

He wanted to sit well forward, which we did, in the seats behind the bulkhead of the first-class compartment. The plane was only half full and the rest of the passengers were bunched at the back, presumably on the theory that the nose would hit first. Faulty logic, said Arbuthnot. The thing to prepare for was a forced landing, when the major hazard was fire. Fire started in the engines, and this little baby had hers in the tail.

Arbuthnot's analysis had one supporter, an Englishman who came up the aisle and sat in the window seat opposite. Given a choice, I'd have sided with the majority.

My own plan for coping with the terrors of flight is to sleep, but this was not to be. Arbuthnot wanted to drink, which seemed a sensible alternative, and as soon as we were off the ground he summoned the air hostess. I explained my financial predicament but he waved it aside.

'On me, man.'

The girl had appeared with a trolley, glasses on top, cigarettes and bottles underneath. Arbuthnot gutted it, stuffing his airline bag with gin, then discovered he was over the duty-free allowance and parked a bottle with me. I began to like him. We discussed old times with increasing warmth, the days when a game of poker would last all night. I still couldn't place him, but that was not surprising. Those all-night games had attracted a lot of suckers, mostly Americans and the sons of sheikhs, who got stripped and didn't come back.

However I studied him closely and was able to give a fair description of him later. He was dark and short and I suppose his eyes were brown, though that was hard to tell since he was wearing tinted glasses. He'd grown his hair long, but it wasn't a success, the bald patch still showed and his sideburns had turned grey as they spread down his cheeks. His appearance was generally hirsute. The sheepskin coat was colourfully embroidered, with a fringe of dirty wool protruding all round the edge. He was roughly the same age as me but wearing less well, bulging at the belt and short of breath. I told him he should give up smoking but he said it would make him eat, which was probably true. He looked a self-indulgent sort of chap. He had

19

studied chemistry at Oxford and had worked at one time for Trans-Equatorial.

That was a coincidence. I told him about the book. He said he would like to read it and we arranged to get in touch – at least I gave him my card and he said he would ring me.

He ordered more drinks, and at some stage I asked him what he was doing now.

'Looking around,' he said.

'You're not working?'

For some reason that made him laugh. He laughed a lot. 'Got a few things lined up,' he said.

'Will you stay in London?'

'I might just do that. London's a nice place, I like it, I really like it. What about you?'

'I like it too.'

'I mean, like, what do you do? For bread, you know?'

'I'm a journalist. Freelance.'

'That's it, man. Freelance. Stay loose.'

He smiled all the time and talked extremely slowly, in a soft drawl, building simple propositions brick by brick. He seemed half asleep. He had obviously made an effort to keep up with the times. Nobody had talked or dressed like that at Oxford.

'Amsterdam's nice,' I said.

'Great,' he said, 'a great city. I really like Amsterdam . . . '

I must have dropped off, because the next thing I knew the air hostess was telling me to put on my safety belt. Arbuthnot wasn't in his seat, but when he came back we agreed to share a taxi into London.

'It's good to see you again, Stuart, it really is.'

'You too, Henry.'

'Still play poker?'

'Now and then.'

'Remember the old Mississippi High Low? Man, what a game.'

'It's a long time ago,' I said and turned my attention to landing the plane. The pilot was a total amateur, letting down the wheels with a thump and messing about with the engine speed, trying to touch down in the suburbs . . .

20

But he made it, and the music came on. Laughing with relief, we were herded into the terminal.

Waiting for our luggage to appear on the conveyor belt Arbuthnot and I agreed that the first man away would go for a taxi, and the last I saw of him he was walking boldly through the door marked NOTHING TO DECLARE. As soon as my own case arrived I followed him. I was through the door and into the concourse, driving a path through the tribes of Pakistanis, when I felt a hand on my arm. It belonged to a Customs officer.

'Excuse me, sir, would you come with me?'

He took me into a small room where a man in plain clothes was waiting.

'What's going on?' I said, but got no response.

The Customs Officer went into the traditional routine, my luggage on a table between us. He flipped through my passport, then passed it to the man in plain clothes and said, 'You've come from Amsterdam?'

'Yes.'

'Is this your luggage?'

'Yes.'

'Nothing else?'

'No.'

'One suitcase, one airline bag,' he said, as if dictating, and held up a board with the rules written on it. 'Have you read this before?'

'Yes.'

'Have you anything to declare?'

'Er . . . yes,' I said, 'this,' and took Arbuthnot's bottle from my bag, a peculiar stoneware object shaped like a cylinder of gas.

He picked it up and rotated it, looking at the labels. He was a Scot, a ginger-haired thin-lipped man with a face as official as a Government White Paper. 'What's this?' he said.

'Bols.'

'I beg your pardon?'

'Bols. It's Dutch gin.'

'Dutch gin. I see.' He looked at me as if I'd raped his daughter. 'Where did you buy it?'

To save time, I decided to simplify the facts. 'On the plane,' I said.

'On the plane. I see. Is this for your own consumption?'

'No, it's a present.'

'A present. I see. Who for?'

'My mother.'

'Your mother likes Dutch gin, does she?'

'Lives on it.'

'I see.'

He passed the bottle to the man in plain clothes, who said, 'I'm afraid we shall have to open this, sir.'

'Go ahead,' I said, 'take a nip.'

Nobody laughed.

'Would you empty your pockets please,' said the Customs Officer, 'and place the contents on this table?'

'Er . . . look,' I said, 'is this really necessary?'

'I'm afraid so.'

'But I've got a friend waiting at the taxi rank.'

While I emptied my pockets they sent a man to look for Arbuthnot, but he'd gone. I began to feel uneasy, particularly when the Customs Officer handed me a list of the contents of my pockets.

'Please read this through,' he said, 'then sign it and take off your clothes.'

The whole procedure took about an hour. They even, in the nicest possible way, shone a torch up my bum. Brutality there was not. While I got dressed they repacked my luggage, then the man in plain clothes reappeared, carrying my passport and a sample taken from the Bols.

'Mr Harris,' he said, 'my name is Carver. I'm a police officer.'

He certainly looked the part. Picking up my suitcase I said with a smile, 'I suppose you're going to arrest me.'

'That's right, sir.'

To boggle would have been the appropriate reaction. But I couldn't stop smiling. 'What for?' I said.

'Possession of controlled drugs with intent to supply in contravention of the Misuse of Drugs Act 1971. Please remember that anything you say can be used in evidence.'

I got rid of the smile. He asked me if I'd like to make a statement.

'I want to ask a question.'

'Go ahead.'

'Where are the drugs?'

'In here,' he said expressionlessly, and patted the Bols.

'That's gin.'

'No it's not, Mr Harris. It's Lysergic Acid Diethylamide.'

'You're joking.'

'Our tests indicate that the solution in this bottle contains sufficient LSD for fifty thousand doses.'

They took me to West Drayton Police Station, where I made a statement, then they locked me up and gave me egg and chips. I couldn't eat it. The cell had walls of white tiles and a concrete floor which rose in one corner to a platform with a mattress on it. There were no sharp angles anywhere and the bedding was the only detachable object in the room, which I took to be precautions against suicide. At least it wasn't cold – in fact the air was stiflingly warm. Nor could I complain of unkindness; I was treated with the sort of forced joviality you get in hospitals. They allowed me to telephone my aunt and gave me the run of the station library, a shelf of well-thumbed paperbacks mostly on the subject of crime. Towards midnight the duty sergeant brought me tea in a large enamel mug and the lights were turned low. I was exhausted but quite unable to sleep. Lying on the bed in the faint orange glow I searched the performance of Henry Arbuthnot for a mistake, and could find only one. Our school had never played Mississippi High Low.

4   Mayer

The police said the name Arbuthnot wasn't even on the passenger list. The more I thought about him the cleverer he seemed. He had told me nothing about himself. The things I could remember were his hairstyle, his coat and his glasses, and by now he'd have ditched them all. Never mind. Once I was out I would find the bastard . . .

But as the night wore on the chances of that seemed increasingly dim. The police said the stuff in the bottle was worth £8,000. If the game was that big, Arbuthnot would be careful to cover his tracks.

And what would I get if they found me guilty? Ten years, maybe more?

No, it was preposterous. I was Harris, freelance journalist. No one who knew me would believe for a minute that I smuggled drugs. My story was obviously true, my sincerity apparent. Of course it was unlikely: the truth was like that. Only liars and perjurers sound pat, as the judge would know.

I lay awake all night, veering from despair to hope, but by the morning the gloomier picture had taken hold.

'You've made the front page,' said the fuzz who brought me breakfast, handing me the racing edition of a London evening paper. I read:

LSD: YARD'S AIRPORT SWOOP

A journalist, Stuart Harris, was held by police at London Airport last night following the discovery of a 'massive' supply of the drug LSD. He will appear in court today.

It was short, but that was the only good thing about it. It would not enhance my reputation in Fleet Street or look good in the blurb of my book. Even if acquitted I would be an object of suspicion. Where there's smoke there's fire, people would say. Lock up your daughters, here comes Harris the dope fiend.

Such dismal thoughts were still in my mind as I was ushered into the dock at the Magistrate's Court. Once more I told my story, and at second hearing it sounded even more implausible, particularly when the Customs Officer gave a verbatim account of my repartee about the gin for my mother.

I was committed for trial and let out on bail, provided by my Cornwall aunt, who drove through the night to my aid. Of such is the Harris stock. As I handed in my passport to the police they gave me a piece of paper.

'Will you ring this number? It's urgent.'

It was the Bosanquet number. Despite my sleepless state I recognized it, and the thought of the name did something to buck me up. Bosanquet – he would know what to do. He would know lawyers. I said good-bye to my aunt and rang from a call-box outside the court. Mrs Bosanquet answered.

'Walter's just this minute left for his American lecture tour, but he said to tell you that he's read the thing in the paper and he's spoken to his lawyer Tony Mayer, and you're to ring him.'

She gave me the number. I mumbled my thanks and rang off. Mayer – the name was familiar. Good old Bosie. What it was to have friends in high places. Finding I was out of change I walked to the nearest pub, where a large Scotch combined with the prospect of a good lawyer restored my morale.

I telephoned Mayer from an alcove in the saloon bar. His receptionist had obviously been primed and I was put straight through, even though Mayer was on another line.

'Harris? Just hold on a minute will you, Sir Nicholas . . . Harris, can you come and see me at two thirty?'

'Er . . . yes . . . right.' The speed of it all took me aback.

'Saint Peter's Court, Gray's Inn, two thirty. Right?'

He rang off. By the time I had got into town and grabbed some lunch I would just about make it.

The sun was shining as I came out of the pub. It was a dry clean frosty day and I began to feel happier. I took the tube to Holborn. As the doors slid shut and the train glided away the whole episode – the airport, the police station, the court – began to seem more and more dreamlike and unreal, until a man sitting opposite drew from his pocket a copy of the evening paper and I saw it again – LSD: YARD'S AIRPORT SWOOP.

Mayer's offices were in a little Georgian cul-de-sac off Gray's Inn Road. I went through an archway into a cobbled courtyard, rather like a miniature quadrangle in an Oxford college. The place was obviously a hive of legal activity and it was some time before I located the plate inscribed MAYER AND CONSTABLE, SOLICITORS AND COMMISSIONERS FOR OATHS amidst a mass of similar combinations jostling for pride of place at the doorway. I climbed the bare stone staircase, its steps worn by the feet of countless lawyers and their clients, and was inevitably reminded of Dickens. But inside Mayer's office the comforts of the twentieth century reasserted themselves: the grey stone flags gave way to a plush wall-to-wall and the dim fog of the stairway to bright electric light. There was nothing old-fashioned about the receptionist either. She wouldn't have looked out of place in a Dior spring collection. She took my coat and asked me to wait. I sank into a black leather sofa and began to take stock of my surroundings. The place was beautifully furnished: there were Daumier cartoons of lawyers liberally scattered about, as if to demonstrate to the visitor a healthy air of self-mockery, and the walls were lined with books, not just Law Reports but works of general reference, history and even a few novels. My eye lighted on the book in which I'd looked up Bosanquet, and out of idle curiosity I took it down, found Mayer in the index and was referred to page 674. I read:

Anthony Mayer typifies a new kind of lawyer who has emerged, staking his claim in the corporate world and prepared to deal with any business, including tax, pensions and hire purchase. A brilliantly clever man whose range of learning frequently staggers clients who expect a solicitor to be little better than a bank clerk, he made his name as the 'Actors' Lawyer' in the fifties, representing famous film stars and theatrical knights in well-publicized divorce and breach-of-contract cases. His influence and reputation grew until he now numbers among his clients city tycoons, front-bench politicians and newspaper proprietors. He sits on countless boards, and is probably the only prominent solicitor to prepare his briefs to the sound of Brahms. A bachelor . . .

I looked up as the door opened.

'Harris?'

I could now pursue my researches at first hand. A small, dark-eyed man of about fifty with a thick, rather voluptuous mouth had emerged and was inviting me in with a wide embracing gesture of his arm.

I jumped to my feet, dropping the book, and followed him into a huge room more like a living-room than an office with high windows looking out over Gray's Inn, deep red curtains and the largest collection of long-playing records I have ever seen outside a shop, stacked neatly in alphabetical order along one whole wall.

26

Mayer had parked himself the other side of a big antique desk and was lighting a pipe when the intercom buzzed. He gave me an apologetic smile and waved me into a chair. There was an odd, schoolboyish charm about him.

'No, Venetia, I do not want to speak to the sodding *Times*. Tell them I'm at an important conference.' He winked at me. 'And don't put any more calls through until you hear from me, okay?'

He leant back in his chair and lit his pipe. It is not a habit I approve of normally but with Mayer I was prepared to make an exception. I noticed now how countrified he looked with his pipe, shaggy hair and thick tweed suit.

'So you're a friend of Walter Bosanquet's,' he said, puffing away like a steam engine.

'Well, not exactly . . .'

'You couldn't have a better friend,' he went on, ignoring my disclaimer. 'Bosanquet will be Prime Minister within five years.'

He pushed a leather-bound cigarette box absent-mindedly towards me.

'People say Sassoon will get the Labour Leadership when Peck resigns, Sassoon or Lloyd-Hughes. But Sassoon is a sick man. I happen to know that, we share a doctor. And Lloyd-Hughes would never get the Trade Unionists' votes. That Wykehamist arrogance annoys them, you see . . .' He broke off. 'By the way, are you the Stuart Harris who wrote that book on the VAT fraud?'

I nodded.

'I thought you might be. First-rate, absolutely first-rate.'

He began to talk about the book, which revealed how some European companies were claiming rebate of value-added tax on non-existent exports. It was clear that he'd not only read it but could remember the details. I was impressed.

'And what are you up to now,' he said, 'apart from smuggling LSD?'

'I've written a book on Trans-Equatorial.'

'Really? Doing any journalism? Don't you write for the *Defendant*?'

The man seemed to know everything.

'Yes, whenever they let me. I've got a few things lined up . . . '

'I never know how you chaps get your information,' said Mayer with a laugh. 'I suppose you run a network of spies.'

'That's right,' I said. 'There are traitors in every camp.'

Mayer stopped smiling and pulled his chair up to his desk. 'Well this is a nasty business, Harris, a nasty business. Perhaps you'd better tell me your side of the story.'

For the third time in twenty-four hours I embarked on the saga. Mayer was taking notes, his small, rather hairy hand wielding a slim gold pencil with quick nervous strokes. When I got to the conversation in the plane, he stopped me.

'So he gave you this bottle. What did he say?'

'He asked me to take it through Customs for him.'

'And you bought nothing?'

'Er . . . no, as a matter of fact.'

'You don't drink?'

'Yes, but I didn't bring anything back. It didn't occur to me. Anyway, I was broke.'

Mayer looked at me intently. For the first time it crossed my mind that he might not believe my story. I dismissed the idea. He said, 'So you were used by this man – let's call him Arbuthnot – to do his dirty work for him, is that it?'

'Yes.'

Mayer nodded, puffing at his pipe. 'It's quite a clever trick, I suppose. And very simple. And now you're up to your neck in it.'

'But surely,' I said, 'I mean, I'm not a drug smuggler. Everyone knows that. Look, I'm just a journalist, a run-of-the-mill . . . '

Mayer laughed. 'Yes, but we've got to convince a jury of that. They don't know you, and don't stress the journalist bit. In my experience journalists are not popular people. Foot in the door, eye at the keyhole. Bad insurance risks.'

I wanted to get back to Arbuthnot. 'But he knew me,' I said.

'What?'

'I mean he knew who I was, he knew my name. How did he know that?'

Mayer shrugged. 'There are many ways of finding out such

things. He was obviously a pro. He'd picked you out and did some research before making his play. What I want to know is this: could anyone have overheard you?'

'What do you mean?'

'Could anyone on that plane have heard him ask you to take the bottle through Customs?'

I suddenly felt sleepy. 'No,' I said, 'I don't think so. Oh – wait a minute. There was someone up at our end. A man on his own.'

'Could he have heard you? Could he have seen Arbuthnot pass you the bottle?'

I sat there trying to think.

Mayer went on. 'You see, Harris, let me put it like this. Without corroborative evidence we could be in some difficulty. What we need is a witness, someone who can back up your version of events.'

Outside it was getting dark. I tried to concentrate. 'But how can we trace him?' I said without hope.

Mayer smiled reassuringly. 'We go through the passenger list. Leave it to me. We have our Paul Drakes for that kind of thing.'

'Paul Drakes?'

'Don't you read Perry Mason?'

'Oh, yes. What about Arbuthnot, though? Shouldn't we look for him?'

Mayer pulled a rueful face. 'We'll try, but I doubt if we'll have much luck. He could be anywhere by now.'

I hadn't thought. I must get some sleep.

Mayer got up. 'But look, leave all that to me, old boy. You look as if you need some kip.' He led me to the door. 'And I'll get you a barrister. I think I know just the chap.'

I was still thinking about Arbuthnot. I could see him so clearly in my mind's eye, the bald patch and the sheepskin coat. I could hear his lazy drawl. Of course I could always make my own inquiries.

Despite Mayer's talk of bleak prospects I felt reassured. It was good to know he was on my side. It was even better to know that a lawyer in his league was prepared to devote his time to the affairs of a minor hack like myself when all those actors and tycoons were clamouring for attention.

There was one of them waiting outside as we came out, a silver-haired striped-trousered man with a vaguely familiar face.

'Won't keep you, Godfrey,' Mayer said as he bustled me to the door. 'I'll be in touch, Harris, as soon as I hear anything. Leave your number with my secretary.'

He shook hands, flashed me a smile, patted me on the back. I was dismissed.

5 The *Maggot*

I should have gone straight home to sleep but some impulse, coupled with the desire for gin and sympathy, drove me in the direction of the offices of the *Maggot*.

They lay across my path in any case, up a little Bloomsbury backstreet above a second-hand bookshop. The *Maggot*, I should explain, is what the papers call an 'underground magazine'. Produced by a gang of freaks and anarchists, it specializes in exposés of police corruption and scatological strip cartoons. When not stupefied by drugs they produce some quite good stuff, witness their pieces on the South African Secret Service, to which I lent a helping hand.

The office is a shambles; piles of back numbers all over the place, unopened mail dumped on desks, photographs of politicians with obscene bubbles stuck on them. Needless to say they had seen the papers and I was greeted with mocking cries from Gorton, the shaggy-haired Australian who is supposed to be the Editor. He began to dictate an imaginary news story: 'Today I spoke to the king of a big-time drugs racket whose tentacles stretch across five continents, self-styled freelance journalist Stuart Harris. An ashen-faced Harris told the *Maggot* . . . '

I laughed. 'No, come on, Gort, this is bloody serious. I could get five years.'

We adjourned eventually to the pub across the road, a dark

Victorian affair that had somehow managed to escape the Brewers' Blitz which has turned the drinker's landscape into a desert of Muzak and carpets. Here in a corner I told my story yet again. Gorton was impressed by my choice of solicitor.

'Tony Mayer's a bloody good bloke. He sent us a hundred quid when we appealed for funds. He's a shit-hot lawyer too.'

I was surprised at Mayer supporting such an outlandish cause. Bully for him, I thought. It showed the man's heart was in the right place.

I went to the bar to buy a round of drinks. When I got back to the table the party had been joined by a very striking girl. She was introduced to me as Charlie. She was wearing dirty grey jeans and some kind of Indian smock with little bits of mirror sewn into it. She had fluffy red hair and a clipped upperclass accent. She didn't want a drink.

'You lot know anything about LSD?' I asked when we were settled again.

'Wanna score?' asked Gorton mockingly.

'What do you want to know?' the girl said, ignoring him. She was looking at me with a disconcerting frankness which momentarily threw me. She had wide eyes, pale and clear.

'Well . . . er . . . you know . . . where it comes from, who makes it, that sort of thing.'

'You're the cat who got busted, aren't you?'

The American jargon sounded absurd in such an English voice but I was glad to hear it, thinking she must move in drug-taking circles. I painted a graphic portrait of Arbuthnot for her. Unlike Mayer, she seemed to think it by no means impossible to track him down. She said she would ask around. I gave her my number and headed for home. If I stayed sitting down any longer I would nod off.

Home is a small flat at the top of what was once a fine Victorian mansion in Camden Town. I stopped on my way from the tube and bought a few tins at the supermarket. Loaded with these and my bags, which I'd been lugging around all day, I staggered upstairs.

With a sigh of relief I dumped the stuff on the landing and groped for the key. Be it ever so humble, there's no place like home. I opened the door and switched on the light and immediately noticed a smell of cigarettes.

That's a habit I despise. Ever since I gave it up.

6 Hide and Seek

I opened the window and looked around. There were flecks of ash in the fireplace. He had drunk some whisky and left the top off the bottle, and peed in my lavatory, omitting to pull the plug, so the whole place smelled of ash and pee and Scotch, like a bad pub.

But nothing was missing. As far as I could tell, nothing had even been disturbed.

Small comfort. The worst thing about such intrusions, I discovered, is the loss of privacy. My home now felt as secure as a bus shelter. I never much liked the place after that and moved to Notting Hill in the summer.

I was too tired to think. I polished off what was left of the whisky and went to sleep with my clothes on.

Next morning I telephoned Midgely at Dynatrax. He'd been promoted to the board. He was now the Sales Director, Southern Region, and didn't want to know me.

'Forget it,' he said, 'just forget it, that's all.'

I slammed the phone down in disgust. Though I hated to admit it, the Dynatrax story was finished. Without documentary evidence or a man inside the company I couldn't even stand it up for the *Maggot*.

I turned my mind to other work, but that was oddly hard to come by. There was no discourtesy, no falling off of friends, just a general tendency in editors previously starved of material to find their feature pages full. Peacock wrote to say that he couldn't do my T.E.M.C. book in the *Defendant* because it gave 'an incomplete picture of the company's activities', but he was sending the manuscript on to O'Riordhan as requested. I telephoned Desmond, but the silly old queen had gone off on holiday and left his secretary in the dark.

I made a short-list of agents.

On the drugs matter, nothing much happened for a while. The mills of the law grind small but they grind exceeding slow. Mayer had hired a detective called Logan to track down the witness on the plane and was busy collecting people who would vouch for my law-abiding character, of whom there was a rather imposing list.

I spent Christmas with my aunt in Cornwall and on the Saturday after my return went up to Highbury for the Chelsea match. That evening I was watching it again on TV. The Gunners looked even worse on the box, and to ease the pain I had opened a bottle of very unpleasant red wine. The phone rang as Chelsea got their second.

'Hey, man, you got busted.'

'You bastard!' I shouted, but he was calm. He sounded half doped.

'Okay, okay,' he said, 'you don't know it all.'

'You bet I don't. Bloody hell, Arbuthnot, I could go to jail for this.' I was slightly drunk.

'Look man, I'm sorry. I'd like to help you, I really would.'

'That's big of you.'

'Cool it and listen. I've been thinking . . .'

'Where are you?'

'Who are your enemies, Harris? They owe me some bread.'

All I could think was, keep him talking. Absurd as it sounds I had the complicated notion that the line might be tapped by the police, who would trace the call and catch him while he spoke. 'Let's meet and discuss this,' I said. 'Perhaps we can do a deal.'

'That's what I'm offering, a deal.'

'What? I don't understand.'

'Maybe they don't like the book. Forget the book, man. Stay loose.'

Stay loose! This absurd advice drove me over the edge. I began to plead. 'Arbuthnot, listen to me. I understand your position, I'm not suggesting you turn yourself in. But I need some evidence, anything. The fuzz don't believe a word I say.'

3

Silence at the other end, and I thought I heard his conscience stirring. I noticed that my hands were shaking.

'When's the trial?' he said finally.

'Three weeks.'

'No kidding. Okay, I'll work on it. Stay cool.'

'You can reach me here.'

'Right on.'

He rang off.

Still shaking, I poured myself a drink and called Mayer. It was after midnight but he was still sharp. He said he'd been listening to *Fidelio*. I wondered if he ever slept.

He asked me to repeat each detail of the conversation. He hadn't expected Arbuthnot to be so impudent. I asked if there was anything I could do, but he advised me to stay put.

'We'll just have to hope he turns up.'

After that nothing happened for a fortnight. Desmond sent my book back saying 'Sorry, not for us,' so I tried it on one of the larger publishers. I had lunch with an agent. The Gunners slipped to second in the league.

Then one day, a week before the trial, I got a call from Charlie. She said she'd had an idea and would like to see me, so we fixed to meet that night. Since she refused to talk on the phone I couldn't tell what she had in mind, but assumed she'd found Arbuthnot, and spent the day in a state of excitement.

Gorton had told me a bit about Charlie. Her name was Charlotte Massingham and she owned a substantial portion of Northumberland. She was keen on astrology and acted as a sort of assistant receptionist at the *Maggot*, where I'd seen her once or twice since that first occasion in the pub, a lofty figure with a very loud laugh, dressed in a long black cloak. She was rumoured to have slept with all sorts of people, but Gorton said that was rubbish. She was very particular, he said.

Gorton was a good chap. In fact I had made him my executor. If I got gunned down in the street my bank were instructed to send him the T.E.M.C. manuscript. He thought that was very funny – 'I'll burn it, sport, quick as I can' – but I knew he would see it into print. Throughout this period he pushed work my way, and paid me more than he could afford.

I owed him some copy, so I took it round that afternoon and found him buried in a mountain of galley proofs. He had news. A certain party had been to see him.

'Short guy – dark hair, purple glasses.'

'That's him!' I cried.

Gorton beat his brow with his fist. 'Sorry, sport, I should have clicked.'

'What did he want?'

'Said he was a friend of yours. Asked what you'd been up to, bought some back numbers, and left. Oh, he left a message.'

Gorton handed me an envelope. I tore it open and read the message inside, scrawled across a *Maggot* rejection slip: *Getting close. Keep cool. H.A.*

'Shit,' I said, 'I missed him.' I read the note again. 'And what's this supposed to mean? Getting close to what?'

Gorton was upset. He blamed himself. 'Let me buy you a drink,' he said, and we went across to the pub.

7 Charlie

I'd hoped to catch Charlie at the *Maggot*, but Thursday, like most days, was her day off, so after a couple of drams I said good night to Gorton and set off for Chelsea, walking from Sloane Square Underground.

I have no fixed position on the Youth Revolution but know that I hate the King's Road, all that computer writing and Bauhaus revived, shirts with collars like tropical butterflies and trousers for cylindrical men. They change the decor every year, but it looks out of date as soon as it's finished. As fast as they run, fashion runs faster, so the street has a permanently tacky look to it. I hate the place.

I was outside a hamburger joint called Kweers when I saw him: the Irishman who'd taken me to the strip club in Amsterdam. It was odd. I knew he was there, but I didn't know where, in the way that one knows one has seen a familiar name in a newspaper, which it then takes ten minutes' reading to find. Perhaps it was a trick of the mind.

Confrontation with Charlie did nothing to restore my sense of reality. She was dressed in a caftan and clearly had no time for underwear. Her face was pale, unpainted except for shadow round the eyes, and framed by that buoyant fluff of red hair.

'Hello Charlie,' I said.

'Hi,' she said huskily, clasping my arm and rolling her eyes in a conspiratorial way, 'come in.'

She pulled me inside and closed the door, then kissed me full on the lips. I was rather excited by this, but it turned out she did it to everyone. 'I'm going to give you something to eat,' she said, implying that this was a privilege granted to few. 'Sit down.'

But I couldn't see anything to sit on, so I wandered about while she went back to work in a cupboard-like kitchen.

Gorton had said that Charlie lived in a cross between an Indian gift shop and a non-denominational shrine, and I can't improve on that. It was really one large room, extremely hot and smelling of joss sticks, of which the central feature was a bed strewn with exotic fabrics. The walls were the colour of blood, hung with oriental rugs and pictures from the Portobello market, and the light was red too, coming from a tinted bulb inside a stained-glass lamp. There was a brass pot full of ostrich feathers and a hatstand festooned with belts and beads. The place was packed with Buddhas and six-armed idols, prayer-wheels, icons and zodiacal charts, and I found a whole shelf of books on I Ching. Beside the bed the Massingham parents, snapped on a grouse moor and framed in tortoiseshell, smiled bravely on the pantheist chaos.

There were three black cats sprinting aimlessly about the room. I decided they must be hungry. I'm not too keen on animals myself.

Eventually I sat on a quilted cushion, so big it almost swallowed me, and by way of conversation said, 'I hear you're a mystic,' to which Charlie replied, 'Read yer cards for a tanner!'

I found that encouraging. She seemed to know she was a

joke, which was more than could be said of the crowd drifting down the King's Road. What I can't stand about them is their primness. Having given up everything for sex they behave as if the rest of us were irredeemably misguided.

Supper when it came was macrobiotic, leeks and brown rice on a wooden plate. It was better than it looked, and I reckoned that any calorific deficiency would be made good by whisky, but was quickly put right on that. Whisky was microbiotic. The world was infested with poisons – meat, butter, sugar, milk . . . Sweeping a cat off my plate, I accepted a cup of apple juice.

'You've got something to tell me,' I said.

Charlie sat cross-legged on the bed. 'Not really, it's just an idea.' She lowered her voice. 'You see, Graebner's here.'

'Graebner? Who's he?'

'You've never heard of Graebner?'

'No.'

'Stuart love, where were you *born*?'

Not only was I ignorant of Graebner, I was also the last man in England never to have witnessed what Charlie was now engaged in, the manufacture of a marijuana cigarette. I watched, temporarily puzzled, as she stuck her hand into the pot of ostrich feathers and pulled out a polythene bag of goldfish food, sprinkled some into a heap of tobacco and rolled it expertly in a paper printed with the Stars and Stripes, twisting one end so it looked like a firework. When she lit it, it burst into flames. She blew out the fire and put the untwisted end to her lips, hissing through her teeth as she inhaled. She dragged the smoke into her lungs and held it there, and as far as I could see it didn't come back. Soon she developed pinkeye, and the room filled with a sweet herbal smell.

'That's good grass,' she said, blinking, and handed the thing to me.

'No thanks,' I said, and munched my leeks while she told me about Graebner.

Everyone knew about Graebner. He had been making LSD since the days when it was legal. He was known as Big G and his product compared to rival brews as champagne to sparkling wine. Chased out of California, he had fled to Mexico and had last been heard of in Algiers. He was wanted by every police force in the Western world, a hero to the freaks and a menace to everyone else.

'And he's here?' I said. 'In England?'

Charlie nodded. 'So I heard.'

She inhaled the last of the joint, grimacing as it scorched her lips. It had burned quickly, like those cigarettes of leaves wrapped in newspaper which we used to make at school. I imagined it tasted much the same.

'The point is,' she said, then seemed to forget what it was.

'Yes? Go on.'

She looked at me as if I had just walked into the room, then laughed, a sudden very loud noise, and kissed me again, smack on the lips. 'Know what I like about you?'

'No.'

'You're so straight. Really straight. It's nice.'

'You were telling me about Graebner.'

'Graebner? He's a great man. I mean in terms of influence on the world I'd compare him to Marx.'

'Really?'

'Or Freud.'

Charlie picked up the polythene bag. Oh dear, I thought, she's going to make another.

'The point is,' she said slowly, 'this man you're looking for – what's his name?'

'Arbuthnot.'

'Arbuthnot. Is that his name? What a name.' She started to shake the bag, then stopped and blinked at me. 'The point is Graebner will know him. He sounds like a heavy commercial type, I mean that's a shitty thing he did to you, and Graebner won't dig that because he's not commercial at all, I mean I don't think he even sells the stuff, he just makes it and spreads it around and the freaks give him what they can. So he might not be too upset to see this Arbuthnot get busted. You dig?'

'You dig' was added as an afterthought. Charlie's hip talk was hopelessly unconvincing. She wasn't a freak at all, I thought, just a girl of limited attractions trying to stay young. Suddenly she stood up, as if tired of the role, and dropped the polythene bag back in the pot.

I seized the mood, and said in a businesslike voice, 'So what we've got to do is find Graebner. Do you know where he is?'

'No, but I know some people who do. Have you heard of The Golden Gate?' I shook my head. 'They're doing a thing at the Barn. Someone said Graebner was with them.'

'What are they, a theatre company?'

'Not exactly.'

'Dancers?'

'Not really.'

'Singers then?'

'No, the groups do that, and if they're feeling right the Gate will do a sort of . . . well it's more like a mime, really. They just express what's in the music. It either happens or it doesn't, you know.'

She paused, searching for a final definition.

'They create.'

'Oh.'

'They're pretty far out. You'll like them.'

She cleared away my plate and washed up. I got the impression that under the fancy dress was a rather well-organized person, a stickler for neatness and hygiene. Every object in the flat had its place. When she came back from the kitchen she showed me the photo of her parents.

'I used to be a really straight chick, you know.'

'It shows,' I said.

'Does it? It seems like a previous incarnation.' She looked at the photograph, then put it back by the bed. 'You think I'm ridiculous, don't you?'

'Nutty as a fruitcake.' I smiled, but she ignored me.

'Let's go,' she said briskly, swinging her cloak across her shoulders and attaching it by a chain across her chest.

Charlie's car was characteristic, a bright yellow Citroën, *deux chevaux*, parked at an angle with its bottom in the air. The seats were of canvas. Without heater or superfluous comforts of any kind, it was a four-wheeled statement against materialism. Pasted

across the back window was a sticker saying BURN A BANK
FOR CHRISTMAS.

When we got in, it sank. 'Tally ho! To the Barn,' cried
Charlie, and heaved at the gear lever, which projected hori-
zontally out of the dashboard. We lurched into the night.

8 Valhalla

We drove up to Finchley and took in the show. The Barn is a
disused Army riding school which has been converted into a
theatre in the round. The show was called *Sunburst* and the programme described it as Tantric Rock. It cost us a pound to get
in, but I didn't object because somebody said the money was
for the Black Panthers and I felt I had a bond with outlaws
everywhere.

Inside, the place was in darkness except for a cat's cradle of
spotlights aimed from the gallery on to a central stage. The seats
had been stripped away and the floor was crowded with freaks,
hundreds of them, leaping about to the music. I say music but
really it was noise, raw undiluted decibels, filling every corner
of that circular cavern. To walk towards it was like walking into
a strong wind. When we reached the stage I saw that it was
coming from a pair of house-sized speakers labelled DO NOT
APPROACH WITHIN 20 FEET UNLESS PROTECTED and was
mostly the work of a very fat freak in a solar topee, shaking
his hair and bouncing in his seat as he punched with all ten
fingers on the keys of an electric organ. The rest of the group
had guitars and drums. On the edge of the danger zone Charlie
shouted something which I couldn't hear and pointed to the
other end of the stage. I followed the line of her finger to where
a Negro in a loincloth was gyrating under a stroboscopic light.
Suddenly a bunch of long-haired whites rushed on with balletic
movements, tied him to a chair and rushed off again. He kicked
and writhed, screaming soundlessly as the music rose to a
crescendo. The chair fell over and he hit his head on the stage.
After much simulated effort he broke his bonds and ran off,

one fist raised in the Panthers' salute. The music blared on.

Charlie grabbed my hand and we pushed through the crowd, who were leaping about in a frenzy and punching the air with their fists. We worked towards the side of the building, where entrepreneurial freaks were selling hot dogs and groups of junkies lay inert in the darkness, and followed the Negro through a door marked STAGE ONLY, down a corridor and into a room where the rest of the cast were assembled.

Somebody shut the door behind us, cutting out the noise, and we stood conspicuous in the silence.

The room was small and bare, four brick walls and a concrete floor. It was crowded with freaks, some standing, some slumped against the walls, all looking at me. Nobody moved.

The Negro's chest was heaving, shining with sweat. His eyes were on me, but when he spoke it was to the others.

'I'm getting heavy vibrations.'

Somebody snorted like a pig.

Eventually a spokesman stepped forward, an alert-looking youth in blue denim battledress. His name was Rupe and he seemed to be in charge.

'Hi Charlie,' he said. 'Who's the straight?'

Charlie spoke up. 'This is Stuart,' she said, and when the vibes continued heavy, added, 'Cool it, he's okay. He works for the *Maggot*.'

'What in hell's that?' asked a querulous voice, but Rupe came to life immediately and shook my hand.

'The *Maggot*! Hey, that's great.'

Charlie warmed to her theme. 'He wants to do a piece on the Gate.'

Rupe was enthusiastic. 'That's cool,' he said, 'really cool,' and introduced me to the others.

And a rum bunch they were; mostly Americans, a sort of itinerant commune of performing drop-outs. Some lay alone and silent and stared at the ceiling, others squatted in groups with their legs crossed, talking softly, their possessions about them, raffia baskets and guitars and blankets tied up with string. They looked like refugees from an earthquake and their clothes were the sort which people give to charity, greatcoats and worn-out tennis shoes, woollen vests, trousers with many patches, grandmother's shawls and remedial clogs. Down the centre of their foreheads was a daub of gold paint, like a brand on a herd of long-haired sheep.

They seemed weary. Their movements were sluggish and their eyes had that dazed expression which you see in the victims of war or natural disaster. As Rupe called out their names they nodded or raised a hand, too tired to speak or smile.

Rupe I rather liked. He was their manager, a bright little Cockney who knew exactly where he was going; as Charlie said, 'a together person'. He scuttled about taking care of their needs and kept glancing at his watch, which was the kind worn by deep-sea divers. In the pocket of his battledress he carried a small computer for the calculation of fees.

That evening's performance was over. The Negro had put on a sweater and jeans and was drinking thirstily from a bottle of orange juice, which he handed to me, saying 'Grab some sunshine, man,' so I took a swig and passed it on. According to Charlie the Golden Gate shared everything, even their women.

Charlie was across the room talking to another black man, whom she introduced as Gabriel. 'He's an angel,' she said, which was about her limit as far as satire was concerned, but he did turn out to be less dead-beat than the rest. He came from Jamaica and was trying to save the fare home by singing in tube stations. We chatted a while and then he moved off, humping his guitar. After that I lost track of him.

Two of the freaks were bent over a candle, and their hair formed a kind of diaphanous tent as they held a turd-like object in the flame, crumbling it into the bowl of a long-stemmed pipe.

Later Charlie explained the difference. Hers was grass, this was hash. But the smell was the same, and soon that room was stinking like a kasbah. I imagined the Barn ringed by twitching police dogs, but Charlie said the fuzz kept away from concerts. When the pipe was passed to me she leaned close and muttered, 'Smoke it.'

I took the point, of course. To get access to Graebner we must win these people's confidence, and to win their confidence we must bow to their social customs. I stared sheepishly at the pipe. They had wrapped some silver paper round the bowl, God knows why. In for a penny in for a pound, I thought, and took a puff.

I couldn't taste a thing.

'Breathe in,' hissed Charlie.

I tried, but it wasn't easy. I either got nothing or too much, hot fumes swirling down, and choked. The only effect that I noticed was a scorched throat. When the orange juice came round again I grabbed the bottle gratefully and took several gulps, then passed it to Charlie.

'No thanks,' she said. 'Driving.' She had a mad smile on her face.

'What's the matter?' I said.

'Nothing.'

'Why are you smiling?'

'I'm not.'

'Yes you are.'

'No I'm not. Here, give me that.' She took the bottle and handed it on. 'How do you feel?'

'Feel? I feel fine. Damn it, it's only orange juice.'

'No, love. More of a cocktail.'

I was standing on a hole in the ground. Falling. I knew what she was going to tell me. 'Oh no,' I said.

'I'm afraid so.'

'Mixed by Big G?'

'Yes.'

I looked at her stupidly. 'I think I'm going to be sick,' I said.

9   An Unscheduled Digression

And sick I was; a macrobiotic outpour in the corridor, watched by a crowd of applauding freaks.

'That's it, baby, the total trip!'

'Right on, man!'

'Go to hell,' I said, leaning weakly on Charlie's shoulder, and to her, 'You might have warned me.'

'You didn't give me a chance,' she said, which might have been true but I didn't believe it. She wanted to see me get high. I thought I might have vomited up the LSD, but apparently not; the stuff was already in my bloodstream.

'You won't feel anything for twenty minutes,' she said. 'Don't worry, I'll look after you.'

'Thanks, Charlie. You're a pal.'

We were leaning together, faces close, but shouting. Inside the auditorium the group were still hard at it, sending tidal waves of noise down the corridor.

Charlie put an arm round my shoulder. 'Come on,' she said, 'let's go back in. They'll talk to you now. They trust you.'

'All right. But as soon as we know where they're hiding Graebner, let's get out of here. If I get nicked in this state I've had it.'

The truth of this hit me as I said it, and I wondered what Mayer would say if he could see me. He'd be annoyed, of course; not shouting, just mildly exasperated, having my welfare in mind. Go home, I told myself, leave it to Mayer. But my feet followed Charlie back into the room.

The freaks were having an argument. As ascetics go the Gate were fussy about their comforts, and as artists extremely particular. Rupe was under fire, having just announced that the programme for Paris included a group called Mercator's Projection.

'That's pig music, man.'

'Holy shit! We can't work with them!'

He raised his hands in surrender. 'Okay, cool it. We can take them out.'

'What about the movie, Rupe?'

'That's where the bread is.'

'Yeah, when are we going to make a movie?'

Rupe looked at his watch as if the answer might materialize at any minute. 'That's a big hassle,' he said defensively. This question of a film really had them animated. One or two were moving their arms about.

'What about the cottage, Rupe? We need it to rehearse.'

'When can we have the cottage?'

'How can we make a movie if we don't rehearse?'

'Go call him, man. We gotta know.'

Rupe nodded wearily. 'Okay,' he said, 'I'll be back,' and left the room.

I looked at my own watch. It was midnight. People kept coming and going, exchanging messages and fixing rendezvous; a *maquis*, who went to ground by day and took over the city at night. I noticed that they touched each other all the time, as if for reassurance.

The Gate had formed themselves into a circle, which Charlie and I now joined at different points. I attempted the lotus position, shifted to a wicket-keeper's crouch and finally simply sat. The floor was hard and I felt slightly giddy, but otherwise all right.

Conversation was sticky. The interview approach got me nowhere.

'How do you like London?' I asked them.

'Groovy, man. A great jive.'

'Where will you go next?'

'Who knows? To the moon.'

'What are you doing now?'

'Living, man.'

And so on. Like dropping pebbles down a well. They could talk about visas and work permits, but the rest was silence. They had no political opinions; they didn't read the papers or watch the box, didn't care who won the World Cup. What they liked to discuss was themselves, and people like themselves, members all of the great fraternity of freaks. The Negro wanted to know where a person called Jesse was, last seen in Arizona. Someone suggested Katmandu, and the talk became global.

'Katmandu? No kidding. Steve says Nepal is a bum trip.'

'Where's Steve?'

'He's with the Panthers in Algiers.'

'How about that chick he used to go around with?'

'Thelma?'

'Yeah, Thelma.'

'She got busted in Algeciras.'

'No.'

'Yeah.'

'Man, that's bad, that's really bad. That whole Spanish scene is bad . . . '

It reminded me of drinks with the boys at the *Defendant*, burbling on about their cronies. Cosy, but ultimately boring. I kept waiting for Graebner's name to crop up, but it didn't.

About this time I began to feel odd.

The group were still playing, and that was the first thing I noticed. The music was muffled by the door, but the thump of their drums filled the room and suddenly was thumping in my blood. My pulse beat faster, was magnified. I throbbed to the rhythm. It was not unpleasant. I felt exceptionally alert and benevolent.

The pipe kept coming round and each puff now sent a shower of sparks through my head. I realized my faculties were going. Unless I found out about Graebner in the next few minutes it would be too late. Driven to risk a direct approach, I was going to comment on the quality of the orange juice when Rupe came back and conversation reverted to the film.

My spirits plunged. I decided they were all in a plot to put me behind bars and was inexplicably reminded of my mother's funeral. I listened in despair as they went over it again, when were they going to get the cottage so they could rehearse for the movie, and Rupe, smiling patiently, replied, 'Graebner says he'll be out in two days.'

To Charlie's embarrassment I started to laugh. The slightest thing could send me up or down, and more often the movement was sideways, disconnected thoughts jumping the circuits of the brain. There was nothing to laugh at but I couldn't stop. It just kept bubbling up.

Charlie looked ready to kill me.

'Who is this cat anyway?' said one of the freaks.

I took a deep breath and shut my eyes and found myself floating in the dark, dots and white lines zipping across my vision, like Morse, or fireflies which hurtled into the distance at each thump of the drums. And there was Arbuthnot, turning slowly as he fell away from me . . . I opened my eyes and tried to think. The important thing was to find this cottage. I couldn't for the moment remember why, but was fairly clear that what mattered was the cottage. With a bit of concentration this business of the cottage could be brought to a satisfactory conclusion and everything would be all right.

I decided to have a word with the freak on my right, a girl who kept snatching at her hair and tucking it behind her ear. I told her I was fond of the country.

She turned and looked at me, absorbing the remark. She was bleeding slightly at the teeth. 'The country's a great trip,' she said.

'Er . . . cottages,' I said, and noticed that the walls were on the move.

'Yeah, groovy.'

'You've got a cottage.'

'Yeah, Rupe rented it. We're going to shoot the movie there.'

'Where is it?'

'In the country. Real quiet, you know? I really flash on the country.'

'Yes, but where?'

'Some crazy name – I don't remember.'

'If you don't tell me where it is I will go to prison.'

'No kidding. Hey Rupe, this cat wants to know . . . '

I was yanked to my feet. Charlie had me by the arm. We were leaving. Rupe was examining my face, like a doctor. 'He's really spaced out.'

Charlie agreed. 'We'd better split,' she said, the words coming out of her mouth like tracer bullets, splashing against his chest.

Rupe nodded. 'Okay, Charlie. See you.'

'Just a moment,' I said, 'just a moment, please. I've got a question . . . '

Everyone laughed, and then we were outside the door, in the corridor, engulfed by an avalanche of strawberry ice cream.

'Charlie!'

'Hold on to me. You'll be all right.'

Charlie's hand, pulling me through the crowd. Noise like falling masonry, great slabs of sound crashing from the roof. Outside in the dark a shadow becomes a black man, who smiles, showing all his white teeth, and says good night to Charlie.

47

'Good night, Gabriel.'

'Good night, Mr Harris.'

'Good night.'

Charlie's car, cold and uncomfortable. Traffic lights exploding in my face, and now we are in Belgravia, shiny cream walls like a morgue. Death around the corner unless this crazy woman slows up.

'Hey, Charlie! Steady!'

'Don't be silly, we're hardly moving.'

When I shut my eyes it's kaleidoscopes, like a colour television on the blink, and once a flock of William Morris birds, flying through the night in diagonal formation.

Charlie's flat, warm and smelling of joss sticks. She makes a cup of tea. Music; a tinkling sitar. Charlie is wearing a necklace of bells, and they tinkle too. It's nice to be home.

Charlie's bed. No more music. A candle burning in the dark. When I try to sleep I fall into a lake of molten lava, but Charlie says, 'Don't worry, coming down's the best part.'

That was true, I suppose. Relative to going up, the descent was agreeable. Charlie lay down beside me and the cats settled on to the bed. They smelled of marijuana. I myself was floating high above a pastel-coloured plain, falling all the time but getting no lower, watching the lightning on the horizon. Death, one hopes, will be like this: a painless detachment of the spirit with first-rate aerial views.

Charlie's voice came from far away.

'How do you feel?'

'Better.'

'My God, you nearly blew it.'

'Must find the cottage . . .'

'It's in Wales.'

'Some crazy name . . .'

'Llanfachreth. Graebner's making acid there. We'll go and see him tomorrow.'

I felt her hand in mine, but that was as far as we got. Lysergic Acid Diethylamide is no aphrodisiac. I don't think Charlie even took her clothes off. She just talked and smoked until I was *compos mentis*, and eventually I fell asleep.

10 Moving West

Charlie's alarm went off at seven, a tocsin to wake the dead. My head had become an echo chamber.

While she had a bath I lay on my back and got it together. That was a favourite expression of the freaks and it made good sense in a world where things fall apart. Sunshine, vibrations, flashes; they all made better sense now.

I was worried about my brain, though. It was after all a good one, the product of two bright parents and years spent in chilly classrooms. I remembered how the freaks had laughed when Charlie dragged me away, and thought, that's what it's like to be mad. You behave in a perfectly rational manner and make people scream with laughter.

I got off the bed and tidied myself in a mirror. Standing in that hot little oriental boudoir I looked like an' ad for an international bank. Our Man on the Spot. The thought induced a fit of giggles, more than it deserved, and I realized I had some way to go to normality.

Charlie brought coffee and a map. When it came to the crunch she was pretty efficient. She was dressed in expeditionary gear, sweater and jeans and boots, with her hair tied up in a scarf and a cartridge belt round her waist.

She spread the map on the bed and marked out a route.

'We'll take the motorway, then strike west from here. Are you ready?'

'Er . . . yes, I think so.'

I considered a call to Mayer but decided against it. He would tell me to leave it to Logan and I thought I was doing quite well on my own. An amateur can sometimes be more effective than a professional. Charlie and I had broken all the rules but I had a feeling we were on the right track. Graebner was the ally I needed.

We left the flat and rescued the Citroën from a traffic warden and twenty minutes later were on the motorway, cruising flat out in the slow lane.

4

The cottage was in the Cambrian Mountains, above Dolgellau, a town which is not pronounced the way it is spelt. We got there early in the afternoon and after some confusion, resolved in a pub called The Madoc Arms, found the road to the hills.

At least it started as a road, a thin strip of tarmac crumbling at the edges which climbed from the suburbs through some stone-walled fields, then became a dirt track, twisting and climbing more steeply through a forest of pine. The forest went on for miles. The pines were fully grown and matted overhead, blotting out the sky, which made it like going through a tunnel. Every so often we emerged for a glimpse of brown hills, then plunged back into the murk. The Citroën was doing well, lurching and bouncing bravely up the track, its two-horse engine whining with the effort. Charlie kept talking to it – 'Come on, baby, *try*' – spinning the wheel to keep out of the ruts and heaving at that extraordinary lever, changing down and down again until we were crawling upwards in bottom gear. As far as I could judge she was an excellent driver. She was certainly having fun. I myself was in a state of nerves. The road was no more than a ledge, and on my side the drop was so steep I marvelled that trees could get a hold. Charlie's touch was sure, but once we almost took a dive.

It was the other man's fault. He was coming down far too fast, lurching round the bends without using his horn, a big grey Land-Rover covered in mud. I must say Charlie reacted quickly. She kept her foot down and veered off the road, ramming the bank on her side. It was over in a second. We were flung against the straps of our seat belts, the Citroën stalled, a rock fell on to the bonnet with a clang and then we were sitting speechless in the silence which follows an accident. The sound of the Land-Rover's engine receded until all we could hear was the creaking of pines in the wind.

Charlie broke the silence.

'Bastard! Did you get his number?'

'Er . . . no, I'm afraid not.'

We clambered out and surveyed the damage. As the shock wore off Charlie got angrier. 'Bastard!' she shouted down the hill, and the word echoed through the trees. 'Who do you think he was? Not a forester, surely?'

'No,' I said, 'not a forester. An Irishman. I met him in Amsterdam.'

'What?'

She looked at me as if I had a screw loose, and I thought she might be right. LSD was known to cause hallucinations. My head felt empty, aired out, as if things had been moved around and put back in a different order. My ears were singing, and I still felt emotionally fluid, prone to inappropriate laughter or gloom.

Besides, that forest was giving me the spooks. It was so damn quiet. Not even a bird, as far as I could hear. In fact it sounded like a ship at sea: the whisper of the wind in the rigging up aloft, and here below decks the slow creaking of wood under strain.

I was not strictly truthful with that freak at the Barn when I told her I was fond of the country.

Charlie was waiting for an answer. 'An Irishman?'

'Yes,' I said, 'he took me to a strip club.'

'Are you sure?'

'Fairly sure.'

'So what?'

'I don't know.'

'Do you want to go on?'

'Yes, let's keep going.'

We lifted the rock off the bonnet. It had left a deep dent and cracked the yellow paint work. 'Poor baby,' Charlie said to the car, 'mummy will soon have you out of here.'

When she backed it out of the bank a mudguard fell off, so we put the mudguard in the boot, but the boot wouldn't close, so we lashed it to the bumper with the belt of my trousers and set off again for Llanfachreth.

As the road came out of the forest it forked. There was a callbox and a bus stop, but no sign, so we took the left fork and emerged on undulating uplands, bracken and coarse brown grass, sheep crapping on the road. The views were sensational. You could look around the points of the compass and see several different sorts of weather, here a black sky and there a rainy one, smudging the mountains, and there a bright patch, fields far below spotlit by the sun. Miles to the west we could see the Irish sea, a dash of blue between the brown hills. The weather where we were was dry and windy, with clouds chasing low overhead.

It reminded Charlie of her home, the moors along the Scottish border. 'But this is better,' she said. 'Just look at that.' Her eyes were alight and the hip talk had gone. Charlotte Massingham was back in her element.

I was on the look-out for signs of human life. There was nothing in sight which corresponded to the usual definition of a village, but scattered all over the plateau were derelict cottages, and after driving for about a mile we came across one which was occupied.

'Let's ask in there,' I said.

Charlie stopped the car and we walked towards it, driving sheep in our path. It was a small place, not much more than a hovel, but someone had spent money on it. The roof had all its slates and the stone walls were patched with cement. The windows had been painted white and through the panes we could see red curtains. Somewhere two motors were running, a big one and a small one.

We knocked on the door, but got no answer.

I went round the back. Lined against the wall was a row of Calor Gas cylinders. One of the motors belonged to a pump attached to an orange hosepipe which ran from the cottage to a wooden shed. Inside the shed was a generator, also running, a deep freeze and a stack of empty boxes marked GLASS — HANDLE WITH CARE. There was a funny smell about.

Charlie came round the side of the house.

'This is the place,' I said.

'How do you know?'

'Look.' I picked up a fragment of glass. 'What's that?'

'A test tube.'

'Come on.'

We followed the hosepipe into the house and found Graebner dead on the kitchen floor, his equipment bubbling around him.

'Oh no,' said Charlie.

I felt strangely calm and immediately started to do things. I turned off the gas and went outside and switched off the pump and generator, then came back into the kitchen.

Charlie said, 'Why did you do that?' in a voice like a little girl's.

I looked at her closely. She was even paler than usual.

'Good question,' I said. 'Don't touch a thing.'

'But he might be alive.'

'Oh . . . yes. Better check.' I bent down to take a closer look, hoping I wouldn't be sick. My belt was now an integral part of the Citroën, so I had to hold up my trousers with one hand.

Graebner was not alive. He'd been hit from behind with an iron bar, which had gone right into his skull. There wasn't much blood. His sheepskin coat was hanging on the back of the door and the tinted glass of his spectacles had joined the crust of broken test tubes. His face had twisted sideways as he hit the floor.

'He's grown a moustache,' I said.

11 Post Mortem

We drove back down to the callbox at the edge of the forest, where I telephoned Mayer. 'I've found Arbuthnot,' I told him.

'What do you mean? Where?'

'Only his name's Graebner. And he's dead.'

'Dead?'

I told him what had happened. Then Mayer said, 'Nobody saw you?'

'No, I don't think so.'

He was silent again. Then he said, 'Look, Harris, you'd better get right away from there. I don't want you seen by anybody. I'm going to drive down. I'll meet you outside Dolgellau Post Office at six.'

I had no time to reply. The pips went and we were cut off. I had no more change. I came out of the kiosk into the eerie

53

silence of the countryside. A burst of sunshine dazzled me. Charlie was leaning back against the car sunbathing and smoking.

'Where to now?' she said, as if we were on a pub crawl.

'Dolgellau.'

On the road back down Charlie said, 'Who killed him, Harris?'

'How should I know? It's a pretty rough trade that, isn't it?'

'Nonsense. It's not like junk, you know. There aren't any big operators – just a few freaks working on their own. No one gets killed for making acid.'

She was right. Nobody gets killed for making LSD, and Arbuthnot was killed. So why?

'He was going to talk to me,' I said suddenly.

Charlie gawped at me. 'What?'

Where the idea came from I don't know. I went on: 'Supposing Arbuthnot unloaded that bottle under orders. Later when he read in the papers what had happened he felt sore about it, that's why he rang me . . . '

'Why?' she said, as women do.

'Half of him wanted to tell me who had fixed it.'

She didn't seem to be following me. 'Why don't you talk to Mayer about it?'

We spent the afternoon in a flea-pit in Dolgellau watching a western. I don't remember anything about it. I couldn't forget Arbuthnot – and what was that Irishman doing?

Mayer was at the Post Office when we finally found it, his car parked unobtrusively in the shadows.

'Hop in,' he said when he saw us. Once again I felt reassured by the man's presence. He was so calm. I introduced him to Charlie. He called her 'darling' at once and told her to drive the Citroën back to London and not to breathe a word to a living soul. She gave me a kiss on the forehead and drove off.

It was difficult finding the way in the dark. We took a couple of wrong turnings but Mayer didn't seem to mind. He drove fast and maintained a flow of small talk. He was trying to cheer me up and succeeding.

At last we found the right road. I was sure when the tarmac petered out and the track went on up into the pine trees. Now at night it was oppressive; the headlights lit up line after line of tree trunks, but Mayer's Rover made short work of the journey.

Mayer parked by the cottage, leant over to the back seat and pulled up a vast rubber torch. As he stepped out of the car, he swore.

'I should have brought some boots,' he said. The ground was muddy. It must have been raining when we were in the cinema. Now it had stopped and a cool wind was blowing the moon through streaming clouds.

We squelched our way through the puddles and round to the back door.

'Don't touch anything,' Mayer said. The door creaked open, and his powerful torch lit up the little laboratory.

The late Arbuthnot had disappeared.

'He's gone,' I said lamely.

Mayer didn't hesitate. 'Get back in the car,' he said. He was completely unruffled.

We were half way down the hill again before either of us spoke. Even then I found myself talking in an illogical whisper.

'He was there. This afternoon. You do believe me?'

'Of course I believe you, Harris. Don't be an ass.' He laughed. 'I'm very grateful for his disappearance, honestly.'

'Why?'

'Well, you weren't going to look very good explaining to some Welsh copper what you were up to sniffing round a dead hippie on a Welsh mountain top. Here, have some of this.' He took a quarter bottle of Scotch out of his pocket and passed it to me. 'Make you feel better.'

We were back on the main road now. The further we got from that cottage the happier I felt. I told Mayer the sequence of events.

He said, 'It's fairly obvious what happened. Something must have disturbed the killer at his work. After you'd gone, he came back and took the corpse. Let's try to forget all about him.'

Once we got on to the motorway Mayer opened up and we

were back in London by midnight. He took me to his place in Gray's Inn, saying he had a date with his private investigator, Logan, and wanted me to be there.

Logan must be close to him, I thought. When we reached the flat he had let himself in and helped himself to drinks, neither fact seeming to disturb Mayer.

'This is Logan,' said Mayer. 'Jerry Logan. He's my Paul Drake I told you about.'

My mental picture of the private detective underwent some structural modification. I expected a seedy anonymous little man in a mackintosh, but Logan was large and exuded prosperity. He was wearing a frilly mauve shirt and a black leather jacket – a well-built stocky man with wavy fair hair and disciplined sideburns. Only his shoes looked incongruous; big thick-soled affairs, streaked with mud.

'Ow do,' he said, and shook my hand.

Mayer was pouring brandy into three balloon glasses. Logan took his with a muttered 'Ta'. His hands were large and awkward. 'Cheers,' he said.

Mayer sank back into one of his plush armchairs and began to fumble with his pipe. 'Well, we've got you a witness, haven't we, Logan?'

Logan had taken a notebook from his pocket. 'You're in luck, Mr Harris.'

Mayer was eyeing him with proprietorial good humour. 'Go on. Tell him.'

'Mr John Harvey, passenger on B.E.A. flight 943, November 11th, Amsterdam to Heathrow, will say that he saw a man answering to your description of Arbuthnot sitting next to you on the flight. He saw this passenger buy several bottles of spirits on the plane and subsequently pass a bottle to you. He will say he heard the words "I'm one over the odds. Would you take this one through Customs for me?" and will substantially confirm your account of the conversation, snatches of which he overheard from time to time.'

Logan closed his notebook, with an air of intense satisfaction.

Mayer was grinning delightedly. 'You see what a difference

that makes to our case, Stuart.' It was the first time he'd used my Christian name. I had no objection. 'In a court case involving your word against that of the Police and the Customs, I think the jury could quite easily convict. But now . . . '

He was right. It was good news. Taken with the brandy and the comfort of Mayer's flat it induced in me a feeling of confidence such as I had not known since before my fateful meeting with Arbuthnot.

'I've been thinking,' I said.

'You amaze me,' said Mayer, laughing. We all laughed.

'About Arbuthnot. He must have been acting under orders, you know.'

'How do you mean?' Mayer asked.

'Well . . . '

I told them what I'd told Charlie earlier that day, but Mayer didn't seem interested.

'You see Stuart,' he said, 'I'm a lawyer. I only want to know about admissible evidence. Whilst I admire your initiative in tracking down the corpse of Arbuthnot, it doesn't help us in the least.'

He sprang lithely out of his chair and straightened one of the pictures over the mantelpiece.

'For our purpose it will be best if we confine ourselves to events on the plane. Our story is that you were used as a pawn in some larger game of drug smuggling.'

'But . . . '

'Just let me finish, old man. We don't want to know anything about that game. In fact the less we know about it the better. If the police want to investigate that, as for all I know they may, then that is their affair. We know nothing of that, do you see? We are decent, law-abiding outsiders who were made use of by unscrupulous criminals, right?'

I saw the point now. I should never have got involved with Arbuthnot. Mayer was right.

Soon after that Logan left.

When he had gone Mayer said, 'Useful chap, that Logan, don't you think? He's an ex-copper. If you ask him why he's ex, he shuts up like a clam.'

He laughed and poured me another drink.

It was past one before I left. As I walked down Gray's Inn Road something Arbuthnot had said on the telephone stuck in my mind, playing over and over again to the rhythm of my steps.

'Maybe they didn't like the book. Maybe they didn't like the book.'

12   Some Points for the Crown

'All persons who have anything to do before My Lady the Queen's Justices of Oyer and Terminer and General Gaol Delivery for the Jurisdiction of the Central Criminal Court draw near and give your attention God Save the Queen.'

The usher recites it as if he were a town crier and the Old Bailey a circus tent.

In fact, as all who have been lucky enough to get out of the place alive will tell you, what is surprising about it is the small scale. The spectators, it is true, are remote; some of them cannot see a thing. But the judge, the barristers and the prisoner can talk to one another quite quietly and be heard. This combination of physical proximity and legal formality is disconcerting.

That morning, at the start of the trial, I felt quite bright. The judge sat opposite me, a small birdlike figure with sharp eyes peering out from under his wig; to the left the barristers, and sitting behind them the solicitors. Mayer was there, black-suited and looking up from time to time to give me an encouraging smile. Despite my position I had a curious feeling that I was among friends. I found myself almost looking forward to the proceedings.

I hadn't had time to get nervous, because one of the peculiarities of legal procedure is that having kept you waiting so long you can hardly remember what the case is about, it flings you in court without warning. The timing depends on the progress of the previous case in the list, which can't be predicted.

My own case had been put back a week, then abruptly brought forward three days, taking all parties by surprise.

Still, I had managed to gather some supporters in the public gallery. My aunt was there, also Charlie, dressed for the kasbah and waving ostentatiously whenever I looked at her. Even Burgess dropped in.

I don't remember much about that first morning. The prosecuting counsel, a heavyweight called Joseph Moynihan, set out the case for the Crown. The jury would hear, he said, how I had travelled to Amsterdam, a place well known as a centre of the illicit drug trade. They would hear how on my return I had been detained by officers of H.M. Customs and found to be in possession of 12·5 grams of the drug Lysergic Acid Diethylamide which the jury would no doubt be more familiar with in the abbreviated form of LSD.

The pompus legal phrases rolled out. Moynihan pulled at his wig, grasped his lapels, tied his gown in knots behind his back, stared at the ceiling, in short did all the things that the audience expected a Queen's Counsel to do.

'You will hear what the defendant said when he was apprehended. You may think from the evidence you will hear that the defendant's replies were not such as to lead you to suppose him innocent . . .'

The jury stared at him, two rows of waxworks.

'You will hear . . . You may think . . .'

He had only just finished when the judge decided it was time for lunch.

'Be upstanding in court.'

The judge got up, bowed, and shuffled out. Everyone immediately began to talk, like schoolboys at the end of a lesson.

I felt my first twinge of uneasiness that afternoon, and even then only a twinge. To begin with it was more the atmosphere of the courtroom than anything specific in the proceedings. An innocent bit of badinage, put into the context of a judicial hearing, can take on a weighty significance.

So it was with the evidence of Customs Officer McQuaid, who looked as though he'd never smiled in his life.

'Mr McQuaid, will you tell the court please, what did the accused say when asked had he anything to declare?'

' "A bottle of Dutch gin, sir." ' McQuaid was relishing his role. He added, "It is known as Bols." '

There were titters in the public gallery. The judge looked angry. Moynihan consulted his papers, then looked up. 'I believe you then asked the accused where he had purchased this bottle, did you not?'

'Yes sir.'

'And what did the accused reply to that?'

'He said he had bought it on the plane.'

'On the plane?'

'Yes sir.'

Moynihan paused to let the point sink home. 'Now, Mr McQuaid, I want you to recall if you will: you asked the accused if he had bought this bottle for his own consumption?'

'That is correct, sir.'

'And what did he reply?'

'He said it was a present for his mother?'

'For his mother?'

'Yes sir.'

'I see.' Moynihan twiddled his gown and stared at the ceiling, to make sure the jury weren't missing the significance of this. 'Now, Mr McQuaid, I want you to examine this bottle.' An usher passed the bottle to McQuaid, who gave it a perfunctory examination. 'That is the bottle which you found in possession of the accused, is it not?'

'Yes sir.'

'Will you read to the court the stamped label affixed to the rear of the bottle?'

'The English Disease. Night Club, Amsterdam.'

'Thank you, Mr McQuaid.' Moynihan asked for the bottle to be passed to the jury. The usher gave it to the foreman and it was passed along the line for inspection as though it were an object in a TV quiz.

I was worried. The English Disease was the club I had visited in Amsterdam. If the bottle came from there, Arbuthnot must have gone there too.

McQuaid stood down.

After him came a forensic expert who said he had analysed the contents of the bottle and it had been found to contain LSD. He was followed by a catering officer from B.E.A., who testified that the airline had never sold Dutch gin.

It was at this point that it first occurred to me I could go down. Until that afternoon the thought hadn't crossed my mind. Mayer had been so confident. I looked round for him, as though for reassurance, but he wasn't in court. Not that there was much he could do at this stage, I supposed. Carver, the policeman from London Airport, was taking the oath in a sing-song voice.

Moynihan coughed theatrically. 'Mr Carver, may we know why Mr Harris was singled out for searching?'

'Sir?'

'I mean, Mr Carver, was it a random search? Did you just happen to pick him, "out of the blue", as it were?'

'No sir.'

'You had some reason then to suspect Mr Harris?'

'We were acting on information received.'

'From whom?'

'It was anonymous information, sir.'

'I see. So somebody knew that Mr Harris was in possession of these substances?'

'Yes sir.'

'Someone who telephoned you anonymously?'

'Yes sir.'

'So, Mr Carver, the suggestion that Mr Harris was a "pawn", an innocent bystander, which is the suggestion my learned friend will make, you would regard as unlikely?'

'Yes sir.'

This was terrible. It was completely unexpected. Why hadn't Mayer told me about this? He must have known what the police were going to say. My mind was unable to cope with these new complexities.

Meanwhile my counsel, a man called Granville, shuffled his papers and rose slowly. 'Mr Carver,' he boomed, 'how would you describe the demeanour of the accused?'

'Demeanour, sir?'

'I mean how did he strike you? Did he appear worried?'

'Er . . .'

'Answer the question, Mr Carver.'

'Not particularly, sir.'

'Was he puzzled?'

'I beg your pardon?'

'Did he in other words, Mr Carver, seem to you to behave like a guilty criminal?'

'No, not particularly, sir. But . . .'

'That will do. Thank you, Mr Carver.'

Granville sat down. I couldn't believe it. Carver had just made a number of preposterous statements and Granville had let him go, just like that. I began to get intensely frustrated Why couldn't I ask the questions? Where the hell was Mayer?

13 Consolation

As soon as the court was adjourned I rang him. His secretary answered to say he was at a board meeting, so I went straight home, poured myself a Scotch and tried to think. The events of that afternoon had unnerved me. Who had tipped off the fuzz, and why? I rang Mayer again. He hadn't come back yet. An hour passed, and I realized with a shock that I'd drunk half the bottle. I began to think now of prison. I felt like someone who had gone to the doctor for a routine check-up only to be told that he had a fatal illness. I rang Charlie. She was out. I felt lonely. I wanted to talk. I went out to a pub and had another Scotch, but the place was almost deserted; the tinkling Muzak and the rattle of the one-armed bandit did nothing to lift my spirits.

I felt sick. I should have eaten something but couldn't face it. In the end I went home, and had just decided to go to bed when the phone rang. It was Mayer.

'My dear Stuart . . .'

It was nice to hear another voice.

'I do apologize about deserting you this afternoon. My clerk told me you looked done in. Tell you what, why don't you hop in a taxi and come round here?'

I looked at my watch. It was nearly eleven. I might as well. I wasn't going to sleep much that night, and anyway I wanted to talk to him.

'You look awful,' he said when he opened the door to me. 'Have you eaten? Come through. I'm just warming up some risotto.'

He took my coat and we went through the door I had noticed on my first visit. It opened on a corridor with several other doors leading off it. He led me into a brightly lit kitchen with stripped pine furniture and a Welsh dresser piled high with mugs of every age and size. The smell of the food was very welcome.

'I've just had a talk with Geoffrey Granville,' he said, stirring the pot. 'He's very happy about the way things are going. He thinks the judge is on our side. He's an old friend of his, incidentally.'

The telephone rang in the other room.

'Keep an eye on the nosh,' Mayer said, handing me a wooden spoon, and came back about ten minutes later.

'Honestly, it's like being a G.P. Women phoning me in the middle of the night to tell me their marriages are breaking up . . . Sit down, Stuart. Help yourself.'

He uncorked a bottle of claret and poured out two glasses.

'Look,' I blurted, 'there's one thing I don't understand. You didn't tell me . . . '

'What's that?'

' . . . the police had a tip-off.'

'Oh, that.'

The phone rang again.

'Blast the bloody thing,' Mayer said, but this time was only gone a few seconds. As he came back he was saying, 'Yes, the police obviously can't understand that themselves, any more than I can. I didn't tell you because, quite honestly, I thought the more you appeared the outraged innocent the better.'

At that I exploded. 'Well really! What a fatuous reason.'

'No it's not.'

'Yes it bloody well is, this whole legal rigmarole is fatuous. Why can't the thing be argued on the facts?'

'Because juries aren't only influenced by facts,' retorted Mayer, flushing with anger himself. 'I must ask you to let me handle this the way I think best.'

'Very well,' I said, cooling, 'I'm happy to do that – so long as you keep me informed. I'm perfectly capable of playing the outraged innocent when required. I am an outraged innocent.'

Mayer laughed and conceded the point 'All right,' he said, 'let's leave it there. I'm sorry, it must have come as a bit of a shock. Do have some more.'

He pushed the copper saucepan towards me and I helped myself. Mayer started on his own meal, talking between mouthfuls. 'My own view of the matter is that there was some kind of internecine feud going on in Arbuthnot's ring. Someone was out to get him, which they did in the end, as you yourself discovered.'

I nodded. These were the lines I'd been thinking on myself. Mayer went on, 'I imagine it this way. Somebody followed Arbuthnot to Amsterdam airport, saw him talking to you, guessed what the game was and rang your description through to London. Later Arbuthnot tried to get his own back, with fatal results . . . '

'Yes,' I said, 'something like that. I'm sure Arbuthnot had been cheated, and he didn't know by whom. He was hoping to find out, so that he could pass the information to me. That way he'd have his revenge and get me off the hook.'

Mayer finished his risotto, mopped his lips on a napkin and pushed the plate away. 'Come through,' he said. 'It's warmer in the other room.'

I got up from the table and followed him, pursuing my theory, which differed in some respects from his. I had almost worked it out on the way back from Wales, but the tip-off at the airport had been the missing link. 'I see it like this,' I said. 'The people he quarrelled with must have been rival manufacturers, because their plan was to get his stuff seized by the Customs.'

'Isn't that rather too elaborate?'

'No listen, it all makes sense. The key to this thing is the

Irishman. He took me to that nightclub, and the bottle came from there, which means Arbuthnot must have been there too. My theory is that he was there the same night ... '

I was on the brink of a blinding revelation. But at that point the mental machinery seized up. 'Well, what do you think?' I said.

Mayer smiled indulgently. 'I think you've got a fertile imagination.'

It was very quiet in the room. Outside a clock struck one.

'Relax, Stuart,' Mayer said. 'Things are going to look very different tomorrow. When our man Harvey gets in the dock we'll be home and dry.'

I'd forgotten Harvey. Harvey was the witness on the plane, the man who would tell the court how Arbuthnot had talked me into carrying the gin. I gulped down the brandy. Yes, I felt much better now. But sleepy. Seeing my eyelids droop, Mayer insisted on my staying the night and gave me a couple of pills.

He was right. He was just like a G.P.

14   I Lose My Cool

Mayer woke me at nine with a mug of tea. He was fully dressed. 'The bath's running for you,' he said.

Outside it was a bright day and the old brick buildings glowed in the sunlight. I felt better.

After breakfast, which Mayer cooked, we went in a chauffeur-driven car to the court. We met Granville waiting with a cluster of lawyers, clerks and ushers outside. He said I would probably be giving my evidence in the afternoon. Then I was in the dock again and the usher was calling for silence.

If I thought the surprises were over, I was wrong. I'd assumed that the case for the prosecution was completed, but no sooner was everyone sitting comfortably than Moynihan was back on his feet saying, 'Call Detective-Sergeant Paulson,' and a black man stepped into the witness box.

I thought I must be dreaming. It was Gabriel.

5

'You are Detective-Sergeant Paulson of the Metropolitan Police Drugs Squad?'

'Yes sir.'

My counsel, Granville, seemed as surprised as I was. He had turned round in his seat and was whispering frantically to Mayer. I couldn't hear what they were saying.

Moynihan went on. 'You were on plain-clothes duty at the Barn theatre on the evening of Thursday, January 15th, and the accused was present on that occasion?'

'He was.'

'Had you any reason to believe that LSD was being consumed on the premises?'

'Yes sir. They were drinking orange juice.'

'That is a normal way of taking this drug, is it?'

'Yes sir.'

'And you say the accused was drinking the juice?'

'Yes sir.'

'You succeeded in obtaining a sample of the drink for analysis?'

'Yes.'

'And it was found to contain LSD?'

'Yes sir.'

'That is all. Thank you, Sergeant.'

Granville's questioning was pretty off-the-cuff. It seemed that the prosecution had sprung the witness on us. He asked Paulson why he had made no arrests, and Paulson said he was trying to track down the supplier of the drug. Had he succeeded? For one terrible moment I thought he might say yes and the dead Arbuthnot would be dragged into court, but he said no, his inquiries had been unproductive.

That, at least, was a relief. But I could see that Granville was shaken, and just when he was due to make the opening speech for the defence. I wondered how far his view of my innocence had been affected by Paulson's evidence.

All the same he made a good speech, laying emphasis on my blameless background and lack of previous conviction.

'I ask you to consider, gentlemen of the jury, whether a man like Mr Harris, a man of good background as you shall hear, in the midst of a successful career as a writer and a journalist, whether such a man would involve himself in criminal behaviour of the kind my learned friend has suggested.'

And he had an answer to Paulson: 'As to the presence of the accused at the Barn theatre, I am informed, and I have no doubt that when the time comes he will tell you in his own words, that on his own initiative, against the advice of his solicitor, he took steps to discover the whereabouts of the man he knew by the name of Arbuthnot. All the more reason, you may think, to conclude that he is innocent of these charges. For we can hardly imagine that if he were guilty he would be so foolhardy as to compound his offence in this manner . . . '

It sounded rather tortuous. I hoped the jury were following him. They sat, as ever, impassive. Eventually Granville wound up and the judge adjourned for lunch.

Things started going wrong again in the afternoon. To begin with, my moral tutor from Oxford, who was supposed to be a character witness, turned up half-canned. I should have warned them to call him in the morning. The man was a terrible old soak. He kept making jokes which only he found amusing. I was glad to see the back of him.

Then it was my turn. Granville led me methodically through my story and I was beginning to feel at ease in the witness box when Moynihan started in on me. His first question threw me completely.

'Mr Harris, what is the weather like in Amsterdam in November?'

I had to ask him to repeat it, which he did, slowly, as if dealing with a dim child.

'Er . . . quite cold,' I said.

'Only quite? Wouldn't you say it was very cold?'

'Yes, very cold.'

'I see. And what is the return air fare from London to Amsterdam?'

'I can't remember exactly.'

'I'm not asking you to remember exactly. An approximate figure will do.'

'About thirty pounds, I think.

'All right. Let's say thirty pounds. Now, Mr Harris, please tell the court, what was your job in November?'

'I had no job. I . . .'

'You were unemployed?'

'No. Well . . . yes. I'm a freelance.'

'You had no regular income at this time?'

'No, I had some money . . .'

'How much? Do you recall?'

'Well, not much.'

'Not much, Mr Harris? How much? How much did you have in the bank? One hundred pounds? Two hundred pounds?'

'I don't know. About fifty pounds.'

'Fifty pounds. You had fifty pounds in the bank, and you spent over half this amount to go to Amsterdam. Why?'

'I wanted a holiday.'

'Do you normally go for your holidays in November?'

'Er . . . no.'

Before I could explain Moynihan cut in with a terminal 'Thank you', looked down at his papers, then said very quietly, 'When did your mother die, Mr Harris?'

'Eight years ago.'

'Eight years ago. I see. Thank you.'

I didn't like his habit of changing the subject.

'Now, Mr Harris, I ask you to recall what you did when you were in Amsterdam. You visited a night club, I believe.'

'Yes.'

'Will you tell the court the name of that club?'

'The English Disease.'

One of the jurymen smiled.

'What sort of club is that, Mr Harris?'

'Oh . . . just a night club.'

'Just a night club. Is it, would you say, a strip club?' He loaded the expression with the maximum possible distaste. In the courtroom atmosphere it sounded worse than Sodom.

'Well . . . er . . . yes.'

'Is that the sort of place you often visit?'

'No.'

It wasn't actually. I began to feel angry.

'Now, Mr Harris, let us come to the bottle. You have told the court that it was given to you on the plane, is that right?'

'Yes.'

'In that case do you not find it odd that it carried a label with the name "The English Disease", that is to say the very strip club you had visited in Amsterdam?'

'No.'

'It doesn't strike you as odd?'

'No!'

I startled myself. I was shouting. The judge said, 'Try to remain calm, Mr Harris. You will not help yourself by becoming angry. Continue, Mr Moynihan.'

Moynihan thanked the judge with an inclination of his head and went on. 'Mr Harris, are you seriously asking the jury to believe that a bottle bearing the name of a club which you had visited on the previous Saturday night was given you by this man Arbuthnot, a man for whose existence we have only your word?'

'No.'

Very sarcastically: 'You are not asking us to believe that?'

'I mean yes.'

Blast the man. I could have thumped him. Anyway, I wasn't the only one who had seen Arbuthnot. Our witness Harvey had too.

'Mr Harris, I should like to come back to something I have already touched on. Why did you lie to Customs officer McQuaid?'

'I didn't.'

'Come now, Mr Harris' – shuffling his documents – ' "I bought it on the plane", I think those were the words. That was wrong, was it not?'

'Yes.'

'You had not bought it on the plane.'

'No, I just said that to save time. I didn't think it mattered.'

'To save time. I see. Mr Harris, you say that this man Arbuthnot knew you but you didn't recognize him. Yet you at no time said to him, "Look here, I don't know who you are," or something of that kind, did you?'

'No.'

'Why not?'

'I . . . er . . . I don't know. I thought I must be wrong.'

'Mr Harris, I put it to you that there is no such person as Arbuthnot, nor ever was.'

'No, that's not true . . .'

'I put it to you, Mr Harris, that your story is a tissue of lies from beginning to end.'

'*You're wrong!*'

I was shouting again.

'Mr Harris' – the judge's voice was icily calm – 'I really must ask you to control yourself.'

I found to my surprise that I was trembling. Moynihan ignored my outburst and the judge's interruption, pressing his attack. 'Mr Harris, you have told the court that your mother died eight years ago.'

I said nothing. I could see it coming.

'And yet you said to Officer McQuaid that this bottle was a present for your mother.'

'Yes. It was a joke.'

I was doing my best to keep cool, but my knees were shaking, I was on the verge of tears. Moynihan's voice was needling as he asked the inevitable question.

'Do you normally make jokes about your dead mother?'

The judge was leaning towards me with a hostile expression.

'NO, OF COURSE NOT!' I shouted. 'WHAT A BLOODY SILLY QUESTION!'

Silence, followed by a buzz of consternation.

'Mr Harris,' snapped the judge, 'if you use language of that kind again, I shall be forced to have you removed from the court.'

Moynihan stood, stooped over his papers, apparently oblivious of this exchange. He waited motionless for a few seconds, then said, 'No further questions,' in a totally off-hand way, and sat down.

Another silence, then whispers all round.

Granville got up. 'Call John Harvey,' he said. Now they would see that I was right about Arbuthnot. I couldn't wait.

'John Harvey!' the usher called.

Then Mayer was leaning forward and talking urgently to Granville. Granville looked very angry. What was going on? I strained over the witness box. Mayer talked on. Granville shrugged. At last Granville turned to the judge.

'That concludes the case for the defence, my lord.'

I can't remember much about what happened next. Charlie, who was in the public gallery, told me later that I went completely berserk, shouting 'Where the hell is Harvey?' and other remarks, that Granville and Mayer had to drag me out of the witness box, and while Mayer hustled me from the court Granville pleaded for an adjournment on the grounds that I was 'emotionally disturbed'. This the judge at length granted, adding that as it was Thursday afternoon he would allow me the weekend in which to come to my senses. The court then broke up in a frenzy of excitement.

15 Getting It Together

I was lying in bed in a small white room, listening to birds. I could hear no traffic. The birds were outside the window, a lot of them, small ones, fluttering about the ivy and chattering after the rain. Yes, it had been raining. But now it had stopped. The sun was shining through the window and something told me it was morning. A fine cold morning in the country, but where I didn't know. I went back to sleep.

Later the angle of the sun had shifted, so the light filled the room, hurting my eyes. I tried to lift my head off the pillow but it weighed a ton. I looked around, squinting against the light. It was nowhere I had been before. A nice room, brightly but impersonally furnished, like a room in a hotel or a private clinic. Good grief, I thought, they've put me in a nut house, I must get out of here. But first I'll have a sleep.

The next time a cup of cold tea was on the bedside table and

I remembered that people had been in the room, Mayer and a man in a white coat, and another man, in plus fours, whom Mayer called 'Godfrey' and I took to be a doctor. My pulse had been taken, my eyelid lifted, and a warm sweet drink eased down my throat. The quack kept laughing, but later went off, leaving me alone with Mayer, who sat by the bed reading a paper. The headline was BOSANQUET TIPPED FOR PARTY LEADERSHIP.

'Good old Bosie, will he get it?' I heard someone say, then realized it was me.

Mayer dropped the paper to his knees in surprise. 'Ah,' he said, 'hello,' then glanced at the headline. 'Yes, I think he will. The party are voting next week.'

He felt my forehead with his hand; a reassuring hand, warm and firm. 'How do you feel?'

'Bloody awful.'

He nodded, his dark eyes full of concern. 'What you need is rest.'

'Where are we?'

'Gloucestershire.'

'Really?'

'Out of reach of your silly girl-friend.'

'Oh, Charlie.'

'Yes, Charlie. If anything loses this case it'll be your little caper with her. Here, drink your tea.' His face had a patient, wounded look. Poor old Mayer, I had caused him a lot of trouble. When I tried to lift the cup he leaned forward and held it to my lips. 'Never mind,' he said. 'The important thing is for you to take it easy, then on Monday we'll go back and win.'

I sagged back on the pillows. A strong magnetic force was pulling my eyelids together. 'Come on,' I said, 'admit it, I haven't got a chance.'

'Nonsense.'

'Complete cock-up. Granville was pathetic – and where . . . Harvey . . . '

'We'll talk about it later. Go back to sleep.'

Sleep – that was the word I'd been waiting for. As he said it Mayer had stood up and put the cup back on the table, looking at me thoughtfully, and there I had left him, abandoning the struggle with my eyelids.

Now more time had passed. The tea was cold, with a milky scum across the top. I got out of bed, taking it slowly. I was wearing big striped pyjamas, not mine. My head felt terrible. I shuffled to the window and looked out. The house was a big one, of handsome mellowed brick, Queen Anne I'd say, with patches of ivy and a flagpole on the roof of the other wing. The sun was still out and I thought it was about midday. There was just enough wind to stir the flag. In front was a garden; lawns and rosebeds stretching to a bank thick with snowdrops, which rose steeply into woodland. Walking on the lawns were groups of men with name-plates pinned to the lapels of their suits, and inside the house I could hear cries and a thwacking noise, as if someone was being beaten with a leather belt. But I kept coming back to the flag. It was white with a scarlet triangle, like the Greek letter delta, and curling up the centre was a snake, also red. I couldn't think where I'd seen it before.

In the corner of the room was a basin, so I doused my face in cold water. The beating stopped, then started again, and I realized they were playing squash. I felt extremely hungry. I found a woollen dressing-gown and put it on, and was about to explore when a man came into the room, a swarthy-looking type in a white waiter's jacket, carrying lunch on a tray. Meat and two veg, treacle pudding and a beer.

'Thanks,' I said, 'very nice,' but he left without a word.

As I ate I read the paper which Mayer had left in the room. There was the usual gloomy mixture of murders, strikes and hi-jackings. Nothing about my case though, thank goodness. There was a long feature by the political correspondent on the Labour Leadership issue. He said there was a growing demand amongst back benchers for a man of integrity, and Bosanquet was the obvious choice.

In the last few weeks he'd done all the right things – attacked the Government for raising school meal prices, given his support to a 'work-in' at a factory in Durham which had later been saved by a takeover, and made what is termed a 'major speech' on the pollution issue.

Turning on from the political news I slipped through the paper, until my eye was stopped by an item in the business section: a paragraph headed 'T.E.M.C.' in a column of gossip about the City. It mentioned simply that Trans-Equatorial had transferred their business to a new merchant bank.

I went back to my lunch, but it was cold. I pushed away the plate and paced about the room. Then I saw it all suddenly.

I had been framed.

But by whom? Who'd pinched my briefcase? Who'd searched my flat? I'd thought it might be Dynatrax. But why not T.E.M.C.? My book would be the first really well-researched attack they'd had to face. Might they not take a few risks to stop it?

Maybe they had planned to remove it altogether, knowing I would never have the stamina to start again. I dislike big companies who uproot native villages, but I don't dislike them enough to write the same book twice. It was just such a thought which had made me put the manuscript in the bank. I was haunted by the memory of an Oxford professor who had left his life's work on a train.

How glad I was of that precaution now! In fact, I thought, I'd led them quite a dance.

Yes, now it was clear. Arbuthnot had indeed been approached for drugs by strangers, who had tipped off the Customs – with one small difference. Their purpose was not to ruin him, but me.

He had seen it at once of course: he had been cheated and I had been framed – that's why he rang me. He wanted his money, and only I could tell him where to look. If he could find out who was framing me and why, some pressure to pay might be exerted. He assumed that the situation had arisen out of my activities as a journalist, so wanted to know what stories I'd been working on. ('Who are your enemies, Harris? Maybe they don't like the book.') Hence his visit to the *Maggot*, and his message: *Getting close . . .*

He must have got too close. Perhaps he already knew the answer and was pressing for his money. But Trans-Equatorial had tracked him down and killed him, using the Irish thug who had lured me to the club in Amsterdam.

Well, damn it, they would find me a hard man to beat . . .

But was I not beaten already? Publishers had melted away, my career was in the doldrums. Even if acquitted I would be dismissed as 'unsound' and condemned to a life of writing gossip for the *Maggot*.

I turned away from the window and sank on the bed, felled by the impact of this new theory. In the end a great deal of it proved to be correct, but at that point I couldn't believe it. It sounded too much like paranoia. Perhaps the acid had damaged my brain, I thought. I would walk those lawns for the rest of my life with a label on my suit, being fed by men in white coats . . .

My mind began to drift. I tried to get it back on course, but it wouldn't respond. I fell asleep thinking of the flag.

16   John Harvey's Terms

Later in the afternoon I was woken by Mayer. He sat on the bed and inquired about my health, and I said I felt better, which was true. The drowsiness had gone. He smiled and patted my feet under the blankets. 'Good,' he said, 'good.'

'What is this place?' I asked.

'It's a business school. I lecture here at week-ends once or twice a year. A chum of mine runs it.'

'The geezer in plus fours?'

'Aha, so you weren't as blotto as we thought. Yes, that's the chap.'

'Godfrey.'

'Yes, Godfrey.' Mayer pulled out his tobacco pouch. 'Where did you think you were?'

'A loony bin.'

His laughter was infectious, crinkling up his face and showing his teeth, which were in good order. He was wearing his country gear, a tweed suit and heavy brown brogues. All his clothes were well tailored and appropriate. He'd gone skiing the week before the trial and was still richly tanned. I thought how attractive he must be to women, with that dark curly hair and a physical grace he had, the sort which goes with supreme self-confidence. But women didn't seem to play much part in his life.

This evening he was pensive, but I was now alert and ready to talk. I asked him what had happened to the witness Harvey, at which he stood up and walked to the window, kneading his pouch reflectively. 'I've been talking to him,' he said.

'He didn't turn up.'

'No.'

'Why not?'

Mayer hesitated, looking back at me as if to gauge the effect of his remarks. 'I think he's frightened.'

'Frightened? Frightened? He should try the view from that bloody dock . . . '

'Now look, old chap' – the pipe was out and wagging at me sternly – 'we'll never get you out of this unless you keep your head.'

'Sorry, I feel a bit peculiar. Did you give me some of those pills?'

'You bet. You were howling like a dervish.'

'They knocked me out.'

'That was the plan.' Mayer smiled and started to fill his pipe, transferring the tobacco from his pouch with amazing dexterity.

'When did we get here?' I asked him.

'Last night. I drove, you slept.'

I vaguely recollected our arrival; wrought iron gates and rhododendrons in the headlights, a helping hand up the stairs.

'You were telling me about Harvey,' I said. 'What's he frightened of?'

'I'm not sure,' said Mayer slowly.

'But without him we've had it.'

Mayer stuck his pipe into his mouth and nodded gravely. 'I'm afraid that's true.'

'Well then?'

Mayer said nothing, staring out of the window. I'd got used to these silences, but always found them unnerving. At least I'd learn not to interrupt, which was fruitless anyway; he was listening to his mind and would speak when he was ready.

But today I didn't feel like waiting. I spoke up. 'You think he's been got at, don't you?'

Mayer glanced at me sharply, folding up his pouch, but still didn't speak. Right, I thought, to hell with it. Preposterous or not, I'm going to give him my theory. Someone's put the arm on Harvey, and it must be Trans-Equatorial.

But before I could utter Mayer took his pipe from his mouth and said, 'Dynatrax. Does that name mean anything to you?'

'Dynatrax?'

'Mm.'

'Yes . . . they make pharmaceutical products. Birth pills, nosedrops.'

'Ever had anything to do with them?'

'Er . . . yes, since you ask, but I don't see . . .'

'Tell me.'

'It's some time ago now. A chap in their head office . . . Midgely. He sent me some accounts, claimed there was a fraud. He was going to explain it but got cold feet.'

Mayer came back from the window and sat on the bed. 'What happened then?'

'Nothing.'

'But you kept the accounts?'

'No, I lost them.'

Mayer glanced at me sharply, then went on as if I'd said nothing. 'This fellow Harvey wants them.'

'What!'

'Harvey gave me clearly to understand on the phone that the nature of his evidence will depend on those accounts being placed in his hand on Monday morning.'

'But . . . that's monstrous!'

'Indeed it is.'

'It's a crime.'

'Yes, it's that too.' Mayer stuck his pipe back into his mouth and took out a heavy petrol lighter. He was calm. 'But moral indignation won't get us far.'

'You're not suggesting we agree?'

'I'm suggesting we haven't much choice.'

'Damn it, I'd rather go to jail. Look, there's something I

haven't told you. I've been thinking. It wasn't just an accident, this drugs business. Someone set it up from the beginning.'

'Now just a minute,' said Mayer, holding up his hand.

'I've been framed, don't you see?'

'Stuart . . .'

'They deliberately . . .'

'Stuart, please. That is balls, and you know it. Arbuthnot was sheer bad luck, nothing more, but he presented an opportunity to this company, Dynatrax, and they've taken it. The point is, the outcome of our case depends entirely on Harvey's evidence. Now exactly what pressure they've put on him I don't know, but don't run away with the notion that we can prove blackmail. They'll have been too clever for that.'

This was altogether too fast for me. I had just about absorbed the shock of being framed by Trans-Equatorial and here was Mayer bringing Dynatrax into the act. In total confusion I stammered, 'What about Harvey? Can't we do something about him? He's threatening perjury.'

Mayer shook his head ruefully. 'It's not just a question of the truth, you know. What we've got to do is persuade that jury, and for that we rely absolutely on Harvey. He's got to be articulate, positive, accurate in every detail. If he hesitates once Moynihan will cut him to pieces. Don't you see? He can ditch you without even lying.'

'Yes,' I said, 'I do see. It makes me sick.'

Mayer lifted the lighter, then took the pipe from his mouth and prepared to make a little speech.

'Look, old chap, I know how you feel . . .'

While he was talking my mind was trying to grapple with the new situation. So Dynatrax were trying to recover their documents with threats – which was a laugh, since I didn't have the documents in any case.

T.E.M.C. and Dynatrax – two crooked companies, acting independently? No, it wasn't possible. Perhaps they were in it together, then.

Before I could work out any new permutation Mayer's speech had captured my attention.

'All right,' he was saying, 'so this man Harvey is making a

mockery of the law. But Stuart, it's you I'm defending, not the law. So for me this boils down to one simple problem – how to keep you out of jail. If I see a way to do that, I'll take it . . '

I let him talk on but I wasn't listening, because I'd just had another shock. That flag on the roof, with its peculiar symbol: I knew where I'd seen it before.

A serpent in a delta was the trademark of Dynatrax.

17   The Beast Within

'Are you all right?' Mayer said, taking his pipe from his mouth.

'Er . . . yes, fine.'

'Sure? You look rotten. Let me get you something . . . '

No bloody fear, I thought, no more of your pills. 'No thanks,' I said, 'really, I'm fine.' I wanted to keep him talking while I worked out what to do.

And I'd just remembered something else: the Chairman of Dynatrax was called Sir Godfrey Rawlinson. So Dynatrax were trying to blackmail me, and here was Mayer recommending that I meet their terms, having brought me half-drugged to their premises and had a good giggle with his friend Godfrey.

So Mayer was a crook.

Lifting his pipe back into his mouth and poising the lighter above it while he tamped the tobacco with his thumb, he went on talking. 'I was saying, we really have no alternative but to do what Harvey is asking. That's why I'm recommending that we go along to your bank on Monday . . . '

'But they're not in the bank,' I said.

'What?'

'The accounts – you said we should get them from the bank. What made you think they're there?'

Mayer blinked. He never did light that pipe. He took it from his mouth and finally forgot it. 'That's what Harvey told me,' he replied.

'Well he's wrong.'

'But surely . . . ' Mayer checked himself and instantly recovered his poise. I was curious to see how long he could hold out.

'How would Harvey know anyway?' I asked.

'He works for Dynatrax.'

'Oh he does? That's interesting.'

Mayer raised his eyebrows and smiled uneasily. 'Didn't I mention that?'

'No, you didn't.'

'I thought I had.'

'No.'

'Well apparently Dynatrax think you put the accounts in your bank.'

'But I didn't.'

It was clear that Mayer didn't believe me. 'I see,' he said deliberately, like a doctor forced to humour the patient. 'So where are they?'

'I don't know. They were pinched.'

Mayer took a deep breath, exhibiting self-control, and looked at his pipe as if wondering how it had got there, then stuck it in his breast pocket. He rose from the bed and began to pace slowly round the room. 'I understand how you feel,' he said. 'It's a matter of pride, isn't it? But there's no need to hold out on me, you know.' He stopped at the end of the bed and turned the beam of his smile on full strength. 'I'm on your side, remember?'

But today I was wearing my invisible lawyer-proof suit. Warding off the rays I said, 'What do you mean, holding out?'

'Very wisely, you put those accounts in your bank. You see, I happen to know that.'

'You do? How come?'

My surprise was genuine. Mayer must have thought I was a wonderful actor. In answer to my question he pulled a folded sheet of paper from his pocket and dropped it on the bed. It was a letter to me from my bank manager dated November 18th, acknowledging receipt of 'the documents' and agreeing to pass them to Gorton in the event of my death. I looked up, but

Mayer had resumed his tour of the room. 'How did you get hold of this?' I asked.

'Dynatrax found it in your flat. It reached me in yesterday's post.'

The more unlikely the line the more casually he said it. He was pacing slowly about the room, avoiding my eyes, thinking on his feet, his brain entirely focused on the task of maintaining the lie, which was proving less easy than expected. Instead of accepting Harvey's terms Harris was asking awkward questions. Harris was pretending he hadn't got the documents. Harris was a worm, on whom it would be nice to tread, but that was ruled out by the tactical requirements of the situation so the only thing to do was keep walking, suppressing all murderous instincts, smiling and throwing out casual answers to each new question that Harris dreamed up.

As the freaks would have said, the vibrations were heavy.

'Very well,' I said, pretending to accept defeat in the matter of the bank, 'let's give him the accounts but make another copy, then as soon as I'm acquitted I can blow the thing wide open.'

I thought I'd got him with that one. I couldn't imagine what he'd say in reply, and I think that for a second he didn't know himself. But in this game Mayer was a master. One could only feel awe in the presence of such talent. 'You'll do no such thing,' he said indignantly and went on with hardly a pause. 'If you do that every aspect of the case will be investigated, and I for one will be in trouble.'

'You?'

'Yes, me. By acceding to Harvey's request I become as guilty of improper pressure on a witness as Dynatrax. And need I remind you that's not the only rule I've broken to get you out of this? Don't forget Dolgellau, Harris.'

'What do you mean?'

This last remark was delivered in a new tone of voice and it took me a moment to recognize it as a threat.

'It was my duty to report to the police what you told me. And perhaps this is the right time for you to tell me exactly

6

what you were doing up that mountain. What happened in the cottage, Harris?'

'Surely you don't believe I . . . '

'I don't know, do I? I don't ask questions unless I want the answers. To me you're a client, that's enough. In return I demand your complete cooperation.'

'Just a minute,' I protested, 'you're suggesting I killed a man.'

'I'm not suggesting anything, I'm stating a fact. If Arbuthnot's death is brought to light you may have some explaining to do.'

His whole manner had coarsened, as if style had gone out of the window with honesty.

'Look, Harris, I'll declare my interest. It's true, I owe Dynatrax a favour. Now I don't know how you got into this but I promise you I'll get you out of it if you let me have those accounts.'

'And if I don't?'

'Then you'll go to prison. And let me repeat: if at any time you try to threaten me, I'll be forced to raise the matter of Arbuthnot's death.'

I told him he was a bastard but he ignored the outburst. 'I want you to stay here and think about it, so I'm going off now and I'm going to lock the door. Don't let that alarm you – it's just that I can't have you running off on private expeditions to your bank manager.' He smiled his old smile, all sweetness and light. 'I'll see that you're fed and come back in the morning. Good night.'

And with that he left the room, closing the door behind him. I heard the key turn in the lock, then his footsteps receded down the corridor.

18   To the Woods

Numbed by this sequence of events I sat on the bed until nightfall, incapable of thought or action.

Then activity returned to the brain cells, and one clear notion formed in my head. Since I didn't in fact have the documents I couldn't even buy myself time, so once the trial resumed Mayer would let me go down, and from prison it would be impossible to prove my version of events. Therefore I had until Monday to save myself. Therefore I had to get out.

If the door was locked it would have to be by the window, but looking at the drop I realized it couldn't be done. There were no handy drainpipes, no sturdy creepers.

There remained one other possibility. My captors were obliged to let me go to the lavatory whenever I asked. It could be that this might offer an alternative escape route. Next time round I would have a recce.

At about nine I heard footsteps, the door was unlocked and the waiter came in with a plate of sandwiches and a mug of tea. He looked like a Spaniard.

'I want to go to the lavatory,' I said.

'Huh?'

'Lav-a-tory.'

'You want go?'

'Yes.'

He looked at me dubiously. 'I go see,' he said, and went out, locking the door behind him. Ten minutes later he came back, this time with a friend. The friend looked equally unpleasant. It was obvious they were taking every precaution.

'Okay, you go,' said the first man.

They escorted me down the corridor to the bog. I made a pretence of great urgency and before they had time to react I was in and had locked the door behind me. It was a vast room with a monstrous mahogany-sided Victorian bath on one wall and the lavatory, equally antique, in the opposite corner. Whoever designed the room had taken care to ensure that the occupant would have privacy. The only window, a thick pane of frosted glass, was six feet up at the end of a little alcove let into the wall. I took my shoes off, closed the lid of the loo and clambered into a squatting position inside this niche. Wedging myself in, I managed to open the window and peered out.

From what I could see I was three floors up in the servants' quarters at the back of the house. From below came the sounds of washing up, the clatter of plates and the distant blaring of a TV set.

But my luck was in. Directly below the window, which I estimated I could just squeeze through, was an iron-work fire escape which descended into the yard below. I was about to make a dash for it then and there when I realized I had no shoes on. I climbed down, put them back on and pulled the chain. Then I unlocked the door and came out, rubbing my stomach to suggest to the Spaniards I was the victim of a nasty gastric disorder. I wanted to implant in their minds the idea that I might have to make another visit, and in this I appeared to be successful as I saw a look of sympathetic concern flit across the face of one of them.

My first plan had been to wait until everyone was asleep before attempting any getaway. But having observed the fact that the courtyard was enclosed by four walls, and that even assuming I got down the fire escape I would still have to go through some part of the house, I decided to waste no time. People would start locking up before long and the last thing I wanted was to find myself trapped by a blockade of bolted doors.

Once back in my room, I started to make preparations. I got dressed then, put the pyjamas on over my clothes. I wrapped up the sandwiches in the pillow-case and stuffed them into my jacket; the tea I poured down the sink. It was probably laced with one of Mayer's sedatives. I felt surprisingly clear-headed and calm. I would probably have to spend at least part of the night in the open, so I'd need all the clothing I could get.

I searched through the wardrobe and the chest of drawers. They were empty, but I could use the dressing-gown as an over-coat. Finally I unmade the bed, took a blanket off, and draped it round my neck. When the Spaniards came, they would find a very sick-looking man indeed.

At half past ten I started shouting and banging on the door. When I stopped I could hear nothing. I tried again. At last I heard the key turn and the Spaniard, the one I'd seen first, came in. He stared at me in a state of alarm. I must have looked odd with the blanket round my neck.

'Lavatory. Quick! Quick!'

He saw the point at once and we almost ran down the passage with him trying to keep a hold on my sleeve.

I was inside with the door locked before he knew what had happened. Once there I took off the dressing-gown, the blanket and my shoes, and bundling them up, pushed them out of the window. I heard them thud on to the fire escape. Before I left I let out a low groan, as of a man in agony. Then I started to squeeze myself feet first through the window.

I slid down on to the fire escape and after retrieving my bundle squatted down and put my shoes back on. I tied the blanket round my waist and clambered into the dressing-gown. It was cold.

At the bottom of the fire escape I stopped and paused for thought. There were two doors. One of them was fitted with a glass pane, through which a light was shining. I tried the other. It was locked, so I had to use the first one. The door opened quietly enough. I was in a narrow passage, white-walled and lit by naked light bulbs. I followed my nose. Sooner or later my Spanish friend would give the alarm, so I had to move quickly.

I was making good progress when I came to a swing door, which I pushed open to find myself at a T-junction. I was debating which way to turn when I heard footsteps, and before I had time to go back was face to face with a stoutish lady in an overcoat, carrying a handbag.

Luckily she appeared more frightened than I was. The only thing to do was to bluster it out.

'Oh, good evening,' I said, with as much nonchalance as I could muster. 'I was just going out for a walk. I seem to have lost my way.'

She didn't say a word.

'Er . . . which way is the garden?'

She was foreign too. But garden seemed a word she understood. She looked at me again and, apparently satisfied that I was not an intruder but just another eccentric guest, pointed in the direction she had come from.

I nodded gratefully and hurried on. I came to another door and through this the lino gave way to carpet, there were pictures

85

on the walls and it was clear that I was out of the servants' quarters. There were rapid footsteps overhead. Perhaps the alarm had been given. Then to my intense dismay I heard Mayer's voice close at hand.

There was a door on my right. I went through it, shutting it quickly behind me, and found myself in a small richly furnished sitting-room with a log fire blazing in the grate. The lights were on and I thought the room was empty until I saw two pairs of shoes on a rug, a man's and a woman's, and caught a glimpse of movement behind the sofa which lay between me and the fire.

With unusual presence of mind I walked across the room, pulled back the curtain, opened the window and climbed out. As I shut the window behind me I saw the face of an unknown man peering startled over the sofa.

I was on a stone-flagged terrace illuminated by the lights of the house. Ahead of me lay the garden. I plunged into it, just as I heard the sound of barking dogs and men's footsteps coming along the flags.

I charged through a rosebed, the thorns tearing at my clothes and skin, then over a longish exposure of lawn till I pulled up short at a high hedge, which I ran along until I found an opening. Through this the grass got rougher and I was going well when I went into a wire fence and fell arse over tip.

I picked myself up, dazed and panting. There was no moon, and as the lights of the house receded the night became impossibly black. I climbed the fence and stumbled on. The ground now ran uphill. Eventually I reached the edge of the woods, turned and looked back at the house. A torch was flashing in the garden and dogs were barking in the distance. I waded in among the trees.

19 Bird's Eye View

The important thing was to keep going, so I stumbled on through the woods stopping at intervals to listen. To myself I sounded like an elephant, but there wasn't much point in trying to keep the noise down. What I needed was distance between me and them.

I had never been for a walk through a wood at night before and it isn't something I would like to do again. The night was black, without a glimmer of moonlight, so I was forced to walk like a somnambulist in a cartoon, with my arms out straight in front to stop me bumping into trees. But that didn't stop me tripping. There was a thick undergrowth, thorny brambles for the most part, and I constantly found myself falling over them, filling my hands with thorns in the process. The undergrowth was wet – there was no frost – and soon my shoes, my socks and my trousers up to my knees were soaked through.

The going was slow. I had the idea that sooner or later I would get out of the wood. It must be part of some big estate. If I kept going I must at some point reach the boundary, a wall or a road. But the wood went on.

After half an hour's painful progress I stopped to rest. It was quiet. Then suddenly quite close came an eerie screech. I jumped. It must have been an owl, but to me the sound was more terrifying than anything I'd ever heard. I am used to bright lights and the comforting purr of traffic by day and night. This dark wet wood full of scuffling creatures and shrieking owls scared the pants off me.

I looked at my watch; it was midnight. When would it get light? I had no idea.

It occurred to me then that I had also no idea where I was going. I seemed to have got away all right, but where was I heading for? I was due in court on Monday; if I didn't show up they would issue a warrant for my arrest. If I went home I'd probably find Mayer or Logan waiting for me. My position from any point of view seemed desperate.

Next thing I knew I had put my right foot in a rabbit hole and sprawled forward rasping my face on the bark of a fallen tree. I sat nursing my ankle and swearing quietly. The wood was dripping. My whole body was wet, my fingers and face raw and hot from brambles.

If only I had a decent pair of shoes. My feet were going numb. Where had I seen shoes for this kind of job? Mayer? No...

Mayer was a crook. The thought hit me like the tree. I'd been duped all the way along. Mayer had threatened to pin a murder on me... Then I remembered.

Logan. He had worn those shoes. I knew there was something wrong about him. Someone had told me once: you can always tell a plain-clothes copper by his highly polished shoes. Logan was an ex-copper and his shoes were muddy. Besides, they were the wrong kind of shoes for him to wear. They were country shoes.

Mud. There had been mud on that mountain top when I went back to the cottage with Mayer.

It was a little clue, but it only confirmed what I now saw instinctively. That Logan and Mayer between them had killed and disposed of Arbuthnot – with the help of the Irishman, of course, who'd steered me into trouble in Amsterdam.

I got up and blundered on. If they killed Arbuthnot why shouldn't they kill me? I was frightened now. The brief exhilaration of getting away had gone. Only when I was sure there were no sounds of pursuit did I slow down.

It started to get light about seven. I felt cold and generally done in. I seemed to have travelled for miles but was still in the wretched wood. The day dawned foggy, adding to the general depression. But as it grew lighter so the trees began to thin out. Eventually I reached a clearing where there was a tumbledown shed filled with rolls of wire fencing and bales of straw.

Inside there was some shelter to be had. I had long since jettisoned the blanket. Now I flung off the dressing-gown, which was soaked. Underneath, my jacket and shirt were still comparatively dry. I remembered the sandwiches in my pocket and

88

pulled them out. Like everything else they were damp, but didn't taste too bad. Then I fell asleep on the straw.

I slept for about an hour and woke up stiff and cold. Outside the hut it was still foggy, and I'd decided to sleep some more when I heard the weirdest noise in the distance.

To begin with it was a tapping noise, wood against wood like Chinese percussion instruments, then, mingled with the tapping, whistling, the kind men make when calling their dogs, and growling, but not the growls of animals.

I was petrified. I stood stock-still listening to this extraordinary assortment of sounds. It seemed to be coming towards me. For a moment it crossed my mind that it was a search party. No, that was ridiculous. I must be miles away from Mayer by now and no search party would make a din like that.

Then suddenly the clearing was filled with a stampede of agitated wild life scuttling through the undergrowth; rabbits, hares and pheasants. I panicked. My animal instincts got the better of me and I joined the rout. That primitive noise was enough to make anyone run. I heard a voice like a sergeant-major's shouting 'Steady on the left' or 'Hold it on the right', and then more banging, whistling and growling.

I ran on. The pheasants were scuttling forward and now and then one flew up through the trees brushing its wings against the branches. From the distance came the sound of guns firing. As I ran the wood began to thin and I came out on to a patch of grass studded with hummocks and gorse bushes which I crossed as fast as I could, hobbling on my sprained ankle across the open space and into the trees again. The fog had started to clear and looking back I saw a line of men emerging from the trees behind me, burly figures loaded with oilskins and heavy boots moving forward slowly but purposefully.

Then I realized what was happening. I was in a shoot, sandwiched between the beaters and the guns.

'Hold it on the left!' came the commanding voice again. The men on the end of the line stopped to let the rest come on. I didn't wait, but ran on into the wood. The guns sounded nearer now and the bangs were coming more frequently. I had no idea what I was going to do. I suppose I had some vague plan of letting the beaters catch up with me and passing myself off as one of them.

'Hold hard to the right!'

A black Labrador came barking excitedly towards me, nosing in and out of the tangled undergrowth. From behind came the barking of other dogs and the urgent frightened whirring of pheasants as they took to the air and flew off to run the gauntlet of the guns. A rabbit scuttled out of the brambles, zig-zagging terrified back towards the beaters, and the Labrador ran after it.

'Steady it! Steady it!' came the keeper's urgent voice, like a schoolmaster's trying to restrain a gang of over-eager children. I was near the guns now. The wood was still thick, tall trees towering through the wraiths of fog, dead trunks lying aslant them and flat along the ground. The ground was soft and slushy, a dense covering of dead leaves.

'Hold hard on the right! Hold it on the right!'

Then suddenly I was out of the wood and stopped dead in my tracks. The fog had lifted and sunlight was breaking through. Ahead of me lay a clearing where the trees had been felled, their stumps still visible in the grass. Fifty yards distant stood the line of guns, their places marked by cleft sticks, each with a white card stuck on it. Beside each man stood a loader, holding a second gun. Pheasants were coming out of the trees thick and fast now, trotting anxiously forward and finally taking off. As they gained height the guns swung round follow-ing their flight. Some were getting through but the unlucky ones, ungainly bundles of feathers, plummeted down with a thud on to the turf, where they lay, still or flapping weakly, until snatched up by the retrievers.

My eye was caught by the man directly opposite. He had lowered his gun and was looking across at me.

It was Mayer.

In the same instant he realized who I was and started forward in surprise, then stopped, still holding his gun towards the ground.

Immobile we stared at each other across the clearing and things seemed to happen with agonizing slowness, like a televi-

90

sion replay, as his arm came up and his cheek closed in against the barrel and seeing him do it I still had time to wonder: is this a reflex action or has he worked it out?

He fired.

As his arm had risen I had been dropping, diving for the ground and turning to flee in one movement, but with some small delay, held back no doubt by lingering traces of the notion that solicitors don't shoot at their clients, so the shot spattered into the leaves behind me. I picked myself up and ran, as Mayer fired again. The beaters were coming through the trees in the clearing now, cleaning up the lingering birds. They blocked the route behind me. There was nothing for it but to run the gauntlet between beaters and guns.

'Stop that man!' shouted Mayer, but the beaters didn't respond, and I even heard one of them curse him for a bad shot as I hurtled past. The other guns were still busy with the shoot, anxious for not a single bird to escape. It was enough to give me the start I needed.

The ground sloped steeply and I ran or rather tumbled down, trying to keep low. The guns were still blazing away and the ground was crowded with dogs retrieving dead birds. I tacked between them, down towards a cart track, running past a startled beater who'd emerged from the trees and was lighting a fag. Parked on the track was a tractor, a trailer full of pheasants and a Land-Rover drawn up on the verge.

I jumped into the Land-Rover and slammed the door. The key was in the ignition.

Snag. I can't drive – or rather I once took lessons five years ago and gave it up when I failed the test. Would it come back to me, like riding a bicycle? No, I decided, looking at the controls.

I turned the key. A red light came on. What next? I released the hand-brake and started flicking the switches on the dashboard, pulling and pushing at the knobs. There were three pedals: clutch, brake, accelerator: I remembered that much. But which was which? I was thinking that it might be quicker to get out and walk, or rather run, when the engine burst into life. Stabbing with my feet I found the clutch and rammed the gear lever forward. The vehicle lurched down the incline, and grabbing the steering wheel I managed to get it back on to the track.

Looking in the mirror I saw a crowd of guns and beaters gesticulating angrily towards me. In addition to everything else I was now a car thief. What was worse, they were going to catch me unless I got some speed up. I had to get the thing into a higher gear. Press down the clutch. Was that right? It was. Now haul the lever down. There was a terrible grinding noise. I tried again, and this time to my utmost relief the gear-lever slotted into place. The vehicle began to make a bit of speed. I pressed the accelerator down and surged forward more smoothly, pulling away from the pursuers. The track forked. I bore left and rocketed on between thick bushes, the odd branch lashing across the windscreen. The wipers were going but I didn't know how to switch them off. Then I was out in the open, crossing a field full of turnips or something, where another gun was sitting alone on his shooting stick. He gaped as I roared past and his dog ran yapping angrily behind. I ploughed on. The track got muddy, the wheels splashed and slithered through thick chalky puddles, then the ground rose sharply and I was in the wood again. I looked in the mirror. The pursuers were now well behind. I was thinking I had made a successful escape when I saw the Dynatrax flag through the trees, then lawns and an ivy-covered house.

I was back where I'd started.

20 Hit and Run

I was travelling across the front of the house, the woods on my left and the garden on my right. The track ran along the top of the bank I had climbed the night before. I assumed it would eventually lead to the house, but kept on down it because I couldn't think what else to do. Perhaps if I just kept going I could drive straight out through the gates.

Then I saw it: a small yellow car, parked on the drive in

front of the house. Immediately I turned to the right and plunged down the bank, bouncing over the unkempt grass, flattening molehills and snowdrops, then thump, a final lurch and I was on the smoother grass of the lawn, skirting half-pruned roses and heading for the terrace past a bunch of strolling Dynatrax executives. As the terrace drew near I considered a frontal assault on the steps but rejected the idea and applied the brakes just in time. As I scrambled up the steps several things were happening. The beaters were swarming down the bank and the guns had appeared at the edge of the wood. Someone fired a shot in the air and the executives, showing the sort of initiative so badly needed in industry today, started to run across the lawn towards me.

I myself was now sprinting across the drive towards the Citroën, as was Charlie, from the opposite direction, her black cloak billowing as she fled from the house, where she must have pressed the bell because the front door opened behind her to reveal a white-coated Spaniard, who blinked in a bewildered fashion then caught sight of me and gave chase. But Charlie was supergirl. She was into that car and had it rolling in no time, accelerating straight towards the executives, who flung themselves sideways in goalkeeper's leaps shouting four-letter words as we passed between them. The Spaniard did better. He got one hand on my door and was groping for me with the other, grunting and gritting his teeth as he ran to keep up with the car, but I beat him off and slammed the door on his fingers and he tumbled back on to the gravel. No unnecessary words from Charlie, who kept her foot down the length of the drive, cornering recklessly between the banks of rhododendron, so we were travelling quite fast by the time we came round the final bend and saw the gates were closing.

'Watch out!' I cried.

'Shut up,' she said, 'and put your belt on.'

She was leaning forward, eyes narrowed as she gauged the gap, a mad smile playing about her lips. I didn't bother with the belt. I composed myself for death.

Someone must have telephoned the lodge from the house. The occupants, an elderly man and his wife, were out in their dressing-gowns heaving at the wrought-iron gates, but their nerve was no match for Charlie's. As the Citroën hurtled towards them they hesitated, then jumped back, leaving just enough space for the car to pass through. Still Charlie didn't touch the brakes. Tyres squealing, we listed to port as she turned abruptly to the right and kept going for a mile or two, until we came to a town where people were about and it seemed safe to stop. We pulled off the road and waited to see what followed us, but nothing did, so we came out of hiding and set off for London.

Once on the motorway we relaxed and had a good laugh. The fog had gone; it was a fine day for victory, sunny and clear. One hand on the wheel, Charlie hugged me with the other and planted a kiss on my cheek. I was scratched, wet, muddy and bedraggled.

'Now I know what it's like to be a pheasant,' I said.

Charlie whooped with laughter and pulled off her headscarf, shaking free her hair so it blew about the car. I think she was sorry that they hadn't chased us. 'Poor love,' she said, 'you do look a mess. What have you been doing?'

We exchanged news.

Charlie's intervention, it turned out, had been based on an almost mystical hunch. She herself put it down to the movement of the stars and I didn't feel inclined to argue. On Thursday she had seen me spirited from the court by Mayer, but had got no answer from his flat or mine, and was rudely rebuffed by his clerk. When this situation continued on Friday she decided that something was wrong. Determined to discover my whereabouts she called Mayer's office again, using the name of a well-known actress, and was promptly given the number of the Dynatrax Management Training Centre in Gloucestershire. On Friday afternoon she telephoned the Centre and was put through to Mayer, who refused to let her see me, saying she had damaged my case enough already. Charlie was indignant, and later suspicious; she resolved to head for Gloucestershire the following morning.

I told her my own long story: how I'd worked out that I'd been framed, the flag, my escape. She seemed quite unmoved by it all, as she had been in Wales when we found Arbuthnot's body.

Only when I got to Mayer shooting at me did she register emotion.

'You mean all those cats were out scouring the woods to get you?' she said. 'That's crazy.'

It was. It must have been chance that Mayer was there. In which case he hadn't known that I'd escaped.

So my pursuers had been imaginary. 'Those Spaniards must have been too scared to report it,' I said. 'They'll get stick today.'

She giggled and patted me on the knee.

'What'll they do now?'

'I don't know.'

She pointed at the cars speeding by in the fast lane. 'They could be waiting the other end, you know.'

'That's true.'

'So we can't go to your place, can we? Or mine.'

'Er . . . no, I suppose not.' I was leaning my head against the window, staring at the Slough Industrial Estate. I felt extremely tired.

Charlie punched me in the ribs. 'Come on, Harris.'

'Quiet girl, I'm thinking.'

But the more I thought about it the worse my plight appeared, the more pointless the night's activities. Mayer had locked me up and emptied both barrels at me, and I had risked my neck to escape: illogical behaviour in either case, induced by emotional stress. For now that I was out, what could I do? My liberty was no use to me and no threat to him.

I knew what he had done, and he knew that I knew, but could I ever hope to prove it? Another outburst from the dock would get me nowhere. Mayer could still have me sent to jail, whence it would be difficult, perhaps impossible, to prove my version of events. The only hand I had to play was the documents in the bank, and that was a bluff.

I decided that I needed some power on my side and said to Charlie, 'We're going to see a man called Burgess.'

21 Burgess Explains

I didn't have any precise plan in going to see Burgess, only the thought that it might be useful to present my story to the *Sunday Defendant*. Also I wanted to know what it was in those documents which so scared Dynatrax, and Burgess was the man to tell me. Midgely had talked of a fiddle in the stocks, but I needed something more precise than that.

We stopped in Knightsbridge, where I cleaned up in the gents' at Harrods. Charlie insisted on buying me some ridiculous clothes which she charged to her mother's account. Then we had a drink in the Bunch of Grapes. By the time we got to Fleet Street I was drowsy. It being Saturday the presses were rolling, a distant rumble like a minor earthquake. Although I regarded the *Defendant* as a waste of ink the sound of those machines brought a tingle to my scalp. Leaving Charlie to park, I passed through the doors and crossed the marble halls, but this time got stopped by the commissionaire. In the end Burgess himself had to come down to vouch for me.

He gaped when he saw my clothes.

'What the hell's come over you, Harris? You turned pooftah or something?'

'I've been out shooting,' I said truthfully.

The 'Background' offices were in turmoil, the floor ankle-deep in paper, phones ringing, people running about. I noticed from the pulls that they were leading with the Labour Party Leadership. Burgess did his best to look busy but in fact had nothing better to do than talk to me. He poured out drinks.

I'd decided to give him my story piecemeal. If I went straight into the events of the last two days he would probably conclude that I was off my head, so I started with the Dynatrax story, describing my early dealings with Midgely and the loss of the photostats.

Burgess nodded wisely. 'Yes,' he said, 'it sounds like a stock fraud. Of course you'd never stand it up without the documents.'

'Explain.'

Burgess put his feet on his desk, hamming up the role of expert. 'As you know, one way to bump up a company's profit is to over-value the stocks. And the simplest way to do that is to alter the figures.'

'That's right, he'd drawn circles round some figures which he said had been altered.'

'Could you tell they had?'

'They looked all right to me, but he said the writing was different.'

'So the figures weren't typed?'

'No, they were lists of goods, filled out in pencil on a printed form. Chemicals mostly.'

'Quantities or values?'

'Quantities.'

Burgess nodded. 'It fits. They were stock sheets. That's lists of current stocks prepared by a physical count in the ware-house. If you can get at those and change the figures upwards the accountant who does the valuation will automatically come out with an inflated figure.'

'How would Midgely have spotted it?'

Burgess thought for a moment. 'He might have noticed that stocks of certain items were abnormally high. I imagine that with chemicals it's difficult to tell. But a fraud like this can run into millions, you know. All you have to do is add a few noughts.'

As with other financial rackets of my acquaintance I was amazed that anything so lucrative could be so easy. 'Aren't there any safeguards?'

'Only one. The auditor has to attend the count in the ware-house. But the rules weren't always so strict, and anyway he only does a random check.'

'So who gains?'

'The shareholders, obviously. A high profit figure puts up the value of the shares, which is handy if you're selling.'

'I see.'

'Is that all you had, the stock sheets?'

'Yes, but Midgely said company records would prove that

7

97

the figures had been altered by two directors. And I'm pretty sure that one of them was Rawlinson, the Chairman.'

Burgess took his feet off his desk, showing more interest. 'That's it then. You'll probably find they unloaded shares. A short-term operation, corrected in the next year's accounts.' He refilled the glasses. He was deep in thought. 'Did you do a company search?'

I shook my head, braving his contempt. 'Didn't bother. Midgely was some kind of Marxist and you know what they're like. I mean respect for facts isn't ...'

Burgess interrupted, pursuing his thought. 'What year was this?'

'1962.'

'I wonder ...'

He left the sentence unfinished. He was going to say something but thought better of it, and to cover up gulped at his whisky. I recognized the face of a colleague who has stumbled on a story he doesn't want to share. 'You wonder what?' I asked, but before he could answer the phone rang.

He snatched it up and barked, 'Burgess,' then adopted an expression of fawning servility. 'Yes he's here,' he said. 'Yes ... no, he hasn't.' He looked puzzled, put his hand over the mouthpiece. 'How did you get here? By car?'

'Yes.'

'Yes,' he repeated into the receiver, 'by car.'

What was going on? Burgess was still talking. 'Will do. Yes, fine ... I'll be up in a minute.' He put the receiver down and stared hard at his desk for a second or two. Then he said, 'That was Peacock.'

I had guessed that much.

'He says whatever you're selling we can't touch it. He's just been talking to your lawyer.'

My heart sank. I felt done in.

'Mayer's on our board, you know.'

I didn't, as it happened. But I wasn't surprised. Poor Burgess. At least he had the grace to be embarrassed.

I stood up and my head swam momentarily. No sleep, no food, and the drink had caught up with me. I told Burgess I would see him around and walked out into the corridor. When I got to the lift it passed me going down; I heard the doors open and shut, then it came back up. It was full of tobacco smoke. Normally I can't distinguish the smell of one weed from another, but this one I knew: it was Mayer's.

I stumbled from the lift and ran across the marble hall out into the street, looking for Charlie. She wasn't there. I ran round the block, but she was nowhere to be seen. Baffled, I stood panting on the pavement. I felt stiff in the joints; my legs were still smarting with scratches.

Then I remembered, I'd told her to use the staff car-park if she couldn't find a place. So I ran round the corner to the side of the *Defendant* building and down a ramp into the basement. It was the usual bleak concrete crypt, dimly lit and packed with cars. I searched for the little yellow Citroën but couldn't see it anywhere. There was no one about.

'Charlie!' I called. There was a sinister echo.

Hearing a movement up the other end I walked towards it, weaving a path through the ranks of cars. Then I stopped, because I'd smelt it again – a faint whiff of Mayer's tobacco on the air.

'Charlie?'

Again the echo answered.

I could see the Citroën now, parked in the lee of a black Rolls-Royce. One of its doors had opened and Charlie's head now appeared above the roof, a ball of red fluff above a white face.

'Over here,' she said, in that little girl's voice I'd heard in Wales.

'What's the matter?'

But before she could answer I saw what was the matter. Mayer was sitting in the back of the car, his pipe clamped between his jaws.

Charlie shrugged her shoulders helplessly. 'I'm sorry, love, They just got in.'

They?

I took another look and saw there was a second man in the car, though I couldn't make out his face in the gloom. So

Mayer has called up reinforcements, I thought, and suppressed an instinct to run. Don't panic, I said to myself. He can't shoot you here, and as long as you stay outside the car you're safe. Go and see what he wants.

I walked forward slowly. Mayer smiled at me frigidly and tried to open the window, but in Charlie's car that was harder than usual. The windows didn't wind; they folded upwards on a hinge. While Mayer fumbled with the catch I bent down and peered at the figure sitting on the other side of him. It was Bosanquet.

22   The Facts

For a moment no one spoke. Bosanquet smiled at me uneasily while Mayer wrestled with the window. Then I glanced across the roof of the Citroën at Charlie, who made a wry face and started to get into the car. But I told her to stay where she was. 'Wait,' I said, 'let's see what they want.'

Mayer got the window open at last, but couldn't keep it open. For once I knew more about a mechanical problem than somebody else, and trivial as it was, this gave me a feeling of confidence. Taking hold of the window I folded it upwards and secured it in the clamps on the edge of the roof. Talks could now begin.

'What do you want?' I said.

Mayer took the pipe from his mouth but before he could speak, Bosanquet leaned across him and said, 'Can we have a talk, Stuart?'

'Yes,' I said, 'certainly. But let's get rid of him.' I nodded aggressively at Mayer, whose expression didn't alter. He was staring straight ahead with a frozen smile. Bosanquet glanced at him then turned back to me, leaning closer to the window. 'I think Tony should be with us. There's a lot to explain . . . '

There was indeed.

Bosanquet then suggested that we go to his house. 'We can talk better there,' he said.

That seemed a good idea. As long as Bosanquet was with us we were safe, and his house was certainly a better place to be than an underground car-park.

'All right,' I said, and got into the car.

Charlie drove up the ramp, turned left and headed for Ludgate Circus, flashing me an idiot grin. I could see Mayer in the driving mirror. He looked tense. Even so it was hard to believe that earlier that morning he'd taken a shot at me. I'd assumed at first that Bosanquet was in his power, a pawn in some devious game, but that didn't seem to be the case. Bosanquet was in command – but what was he up to? Had he tumbled to the plot and intervened on my behalf? I couldn't work it out. I only knew I was very glad to see him.

As danger receded, exhaustion closed in. My mind went blank. I just stared out the window. It was Saturday lunch-time and the streets were almost empty as we went through Holborn and across Oxford Circus. Charlie careered round Marble Arch then straightened up into Bayswater Road. There were people walking in the park, some kids playing football. Mayer lit his pipe and filled the car with smoke.

As we passed Holland Park tube station, Bosanquet spoke. 'Turn left at the lights and take the second turning on the right.'

'Right you are, sir,' said Charlie.

It was all so unreal. I wanted to ask them questions but couldn't think what to say. A wild suspicion had reached the corner of my mind, but I dismissed it as absurd. Eventually the car drew up by the stuccoed house in the quiet cul-de-sac. We extricated ourselves and Bosanquet said, 'Come on in. I hope you'll both stay to lunch?'

Charlie grinned and shrugged. She was getting more like Harpo Marx as the hours wore on.

Bosanquet shut the front door behind us and threw his coat over the banisters. 'I think we'd better go upstairs,' he said, and to Charlie, 'If you carry on up to the top of the house you should find Barry, my son. Ask him to play you some of his records.'

Charlie swung her cloak off her shoulders and Bosanquet

hung it on a hook. She was obviously charmed by him. When we reached the first floor, she went on up. Mayer and I followed Bosanquet into his study.

There he relaxed and waved us into chairs, taking off his jacket and putting on a moth-eaten cardigan. He was a small man, plump and untidy. Surrounded by his books he looked more like a don than a politician.

'Well,' he said, 'I suppose we'd better have this matter out.'

I sat on the sofa, my head full of questions. Have what out? What was going on?

Mayer rose urgently from his chair, one hand outstretched, and found his voice at last. 'Walter, are you sure this is wise?'

Bosanquet's dismissal was ruthless, a glimpse of leadership potential. 'Tony, would you leave us please? I think you've done quite enough damage already.'

'But Walter . . . '

'Tell Margaret we'll be two more for lunch.'

'Very well. As you wish.'

Mayer left the room, like a cowed dog. After he had gone Bosanquet took up a position in front of the fireplace, jiggling the keys in his pocket. That was one of his mannerisms; another was to run his hand through his wispy grey hair, as if it bothered him to have it too neatly arranged. He didn't smoke, I noticed.

'Look, Stuart,' he said, 'first of all I owe you an apology. I won't pretend that some of us haven't – er . . . over-reacted, so to speak.'

He smiled. I said nothing.

'Tony Mayer's a brilliant lawyer and a loyal friend. But he's apt to . . . cut corners, shall we say? He was a prisoner of the Japs, did you know?'

'Oh. No, I didn't.'

'Yes, he had a rotten time of it.'

A moment's silence, in which I heard Charlie laughing raucously two floors above. Bosanquet walked to the window, and talked on over his shoulder.

'Anyway, when my wife overheard you telephone your contact in Dynatrax from this room she of course informed me, and I told Tony, who has acted for me in this matter for several years. I left him to do what he thought best, but I'm afraid from what he's told me that he may have been less than scrupulous in protecting my interests. If that is the case I regret it, and apologize.'

Bosanquet came back from the window and looked at me intently, the model of sincerity.

'Personally, I couldn't care less whether these wretched documents are in your bank or whatever. Do you see?'

I nodded.

'What I want is for you to know the full facts and then you can decide for yourself what you want to do about it.'

The smell of lunch was drifting up through the house, and I suddenly realized how hungry I was. Upstairs Barry was playing his guitar and Charlie, of all things, was singing. Knowing what I did, that I had no documents, I felt detached. Bosanquet went on.

'The first thing to say is that it all happened some time ago.'

He resumed his position in front of the fireplace, jiggling his keys again.

'One of the disadvantages of being a politician is they don't pay you much. And at that time – this is ten years ago now – I was pretty short. In fact I was broke. As you know yourself, you don't make much out of writing books, and we'd just bought this house on a bloody great mortgage, and oh, I don't know, there was a mass of bills to pay . . . Cigarette?'

He held out a box. I shook my head.

'So when these Dynatrax people came along and offered me a directorship I admit I snapped it up. I asked around the City first of course, and everyone I spoke to gave the company first-class references. It was only later that I found they'd been working a fiddle. It's a complicated business which I don't want to go into now. The point is, Stuart, as soon as I discovered what was going on, I got out. You can say I was a fool, but I don't think you can say I was a crook.'

He smiled. I smiled back. He obviously thought that I knew all this already, though Mayer hadn't been so sure. He went on.

'Now none of this would matter very much if it wasn't for

two things. Firstly I'm in the Labour Party, and the members of that party quite rightly don't approve of big business, though in a lot of cases there's an element of hypocrisy in that. That's my view, at any rate. I say, would you like a drink?'

He had opened a cupboard in his bookcase and was pouring a large gin which he splashed some tonic into. This would be the last one, I said to myself.

'The other thing of course, as you probably realize, is that this is a very bad moment for something like this to get out. At any other time it wouldn't really matter. As it is . . . well, the Leadership's wide open, and I hope you won't think me arrogant if I say that I honestly believe I can make a good job of it. God knows, the party could do with a shake-up . . . We could really . . . '

He broke off, as though ashamed at this display of feeling.

'But we don't want to go into that now. The point is – and this is something . . . it's entirely up to you to decide for yourself – if that Dynatrax story came out now, at this point, it would finish me. Don't let's pretend that my rivals wouldn't use it for all it's worth. As for the Tories . . . '

'What about the shares?' I said.

It was a guess, but a good one, prompted by that look on Burgess's face.

Bosanquet stared at me, startled by the interruption. 'I'm sorry, I don't follow. What shares?'

'When you took the directorship Dynatrax also offered shares, didn't they?'

'Oh yes, that's the normal thing. I got rid of them when I got out.'

'At a profit?'

'I really can't remember . . . '

He scratched at his hair, then walked to the window again. This time I stood up and followed him, surprised by my own audacity. 'Can't you? When did you get out?'

'Let's see . . . It was the year before we took office . . . '

'1963? In that case you must have cashed in on the share price jacked up by Rawlinson's stock fraud. How many shares did you have?'

Bosanquet spun round, his face flushed with anger. For a moment I thought he was going to shout, then he regained control and said, 'I think we'd better have Tony back in here.'

Poor old Mayer, I thought. Picked up or dropped as necessity arose, useful for the rough stuff.

My sympathy was temporary. Outside the window a man in a mackintosh was digging in the bonnet of Charlie's car. As I watched he straightened up and slipped something in his pocket. It was the Irishman from Amsterdam. Simultaneously Mayer and Logan were coming up the garden path. They exchanged a few words, then Mayer came into the house.

Seeing the three of them together I realized at last what had happened. Acting for Bosanquet, Mayer had planned the whole thing *purely to recover the Dynatrax documents.* Trans-Equatorial had had nothing to do with it.

I turned back into the room. Bosanquet had moved towards the door to call Mayer, but at that moment Barry came in with Charlie and said, 'Luncheon is served' in a butler's voice.

Charlie cackled.

Mayer came up behind them, immediately followed by Mrs B, removing an apron and adjusting her hair. She said hello to me then suggested a drink, just as Barry handed me a file.

'You left this,' he said, 'last time you were here.'

I reached for the file, trying not to snatch, but Barry, bless his heart, pointed to the word written large on the cover with a green felt pen.

'Make a good name for a group, that would.'

His mother leaned forward, tilting her head to look. 'What's that, darling?'

'Dynatrax.'

23 The Rough Stuff

There should have been a fight at that point. But there wasn't.

We had another drink. We had lunch.

I put the file on my chair and sat on it. Nobody mentioned

it. With Bosanquet in charge the Queensberry Rules were going to be observed.

I didn't pay much attention to the conversation. I was thinking as hard as the state of my head would allow, filling in the gaps.

You have to give Mayer full marks for initiative. His mission had been to recover the incriminating stock sheets, and when his searches convinced him they were in my bank he had looked for a way to persuade me to surrender them. I was not the sort of person to be bribed or threatened; I had therefore, seemingly by accident, to be put in a position so dangerous I'd be glad to trade them in to escape from it. His solution was to frame me on a drugs charge, and get himself appointed my solicitor. Once that was achieved he had me in his power, and could steer the trial towards the point where its outcome depended on the evidence of Harvey.

And what about Bosanquet? How much did he know of what had happened? He gave nothing away. Had Mayer told him about the pheasant shoot? Was that part of the 'over-acting'?

One thing soon became clear: Mrs Bosanquet had been kept in the dark. And that made the situation more tense. She began to question Mayer about how the trial was going. Charlie giggled. Mayer flushed, looked to Bosanquet for support and found none. He stammered out something to the effect that it would all come right on the night.

Then there was silence, broken only by the desultory clashing of cutlery, until Mrs B, perfect hostess to the last, said, 'Well, Stuart, tell us about your book.'

It took me a moment to register what she was talking about. I'd forgotten about Trans-Equatorial. As I groped for something to say I realized that in addition to being dog tired I was more than slightly canned.

I managed to say something, I think. But Bosanquet gratefully took the cue and started to speak about T.E.M.C. and how they exploited native labour in South America. He spoke eloquently about the ruthlessness of modern capitalism. He said in the old days the big industrialists had at least been men of some culture with a modicum of concern about the ethical side,

All this was addressed to me, and very good stuff it was. Taking another swig of his claret I thought that after all maybe Bosanquet was right. What was the point of dragging up some old gaffe which could put paid to the man's career?

As if answering my mood, Bosanquet pressed on. We were all listening now, even Charlie. He got on to the subject of the Environment. I remember him saying how sick he felt when he saw a line of pylons straddling some nice stretch of country; how, for just a little more money, the cables could have been put below ground; how posterity would curse us for a bunch of money-grabbers and Philistines . . .

I found myself nodding in agreement and told him the story of how Trans-Equatorial had virtually destroyed an island in the Pacific in order to get at some copper deposits. That brought him on to Wales and how mining companies were trying to plough up the National Parks.

He should never have mentioned Wales. It reminded me of a cottage in the mountains, the Irish Sea in the distance, and a dead man on the kitchen floor.

His killer was now in the street outside, a piece of Citroën in his pocket.

Bosanquet was still in full flood, but he'd lost me. I was watching a man acting a part – the part of a public figure with his heart in all the sorts of places that I, Stuart Harris, would approve of.

I glanced at Charlie. Her eyes looked somewhat muzzy and the wine had brought two spots of colour to her cheeks, but I knew that she was on the alert.

Barry was mainly concerned with food.

Mayer sat silent and pale. He seemed to have shrunk, a man defeated – or rather a wounded animal, still dangerous, capable of violence. I didn't like the look of him at all.

He clearly had no faith in Bosanquet's approach, and was waiting to apply sterner methods. He had sabotaged the Citroën and posted two men out in front. His original plan must have been to get me locked up again, immobilized until the resumption of the trial. But now, thanks to Barry, the prize was greater: I had the precious stock sheets, and of those he would deprive me by any means necessary. The Queensberry Rules were about to be dropped.

During pudding I worked out a plan. I knew from experience that coffee would be in the drawing-room, which was on the first floor at the back. Bosanquet had said that he had to leave at two thirty for an interview with French Television. Mayer wouldn't make a move till then.

When we rose to clear the table I winked at Charlie and got close enough to whisper in the corridor. Almost on the instant Bosanquet came up with a tray of dirty glasses, but Charlie took it from him, saying, 'Please, let me,' and carried it gaily off to the kitchen. A few minutes later she had vanished from the house. Good old Charlie.

As expected we had coffee in the drawing-room, then Mrs B collected the cups on a tray and called to Barry to go with her. 'You can help me wash these,' she said, picking up the tray.

'Okay. Come on, Harris.'

'Stuart's staying here.'

'But we're talking.'

'It won't take a minute.'

'Do I have to?'

'Barry, please. Just do as you're told.'

'Oh all right.'

Barry sighed theatrically, shrugged at me and slouched off. 'Close the door,' said his mother, and he did so. Now we were three.

The room overlooked the back garden. Some tall french windows opened on to an ornate iron balcony painted white and crowded with potted plants. At either end of it steps spiralled down to the garden below.

Bosanquet looked at his watch. 'Well,' he said, 'I mustn't keep our French friends waiting. Thanks for coming round.' He shook my hand, paused, waiting for the file, then walked from the room looking aggrieved.

Watching him go I felt a surge of contempt for the man, so politely consigning me to the rough-house, pretending not to know. The bold crusader against electricity pylons.

Mayer saw him out, then closed the door and turned to face me. 'Well?' he said harshly.

His face was grey, without a vestige of goodwill. He looked ready for anything.

'Well what?' I said, clutching the file.

He held out his hand. 'Let's have it.'

'What if I refuse?'

'Then I'll have to call Logan. He's waiting outside.'

'I see,' I said, pretending to dither. My plan required only that I be left alone, and now I got my chance. Hearing the front door close I said, 'All right, I'll hand it over – to Bosanquet.'

'He's gone.'

'Well call him back. I'm not giving this to anyone else.'

Mayer considered for a moment, then nodded. 'All right,' he said, 'wait here,' and left the room.

Immediately I tried the french windows. They were locked. I looked behind the curtains, found the key on a hook and got the windows open with a rattle. But Logan had been sent to keep an eye on me. Hearing the rattle he rushed into the room and before I could get out he had an arm round my neck, forcing up my chin and pinning my head back against his chest in a grip of frightening force. He was panting in my ear, his cheek against mine – the horrible intimacy of violence. He flailed for the file with his free hand. I held it out at arm's length, just beyond his reach, and stamped on his feet. Logan swore but held on, so I hurled myself into reverse, pushing back as hard as I could until we both toppled over a sofa and he smashed his head on a heavy glass table. He grunted and his grip went slack. I struggled to my feet and then I was outside the windows, slamming them in Logan's face, clattering down the steps of the balcony and sprinting across a muddy lawn. The garden was the usual London variety, bounded by a high brick wall. Logan was a few yards behind me. He thought he'd got me cornered but I knew the place better than he did. In earlier years Barry had been gripped by a Tarzan fantasy to which the monument was a complex and unstable tree-house in the sycamore against the back wall. Clamping the file between my teeth I scrambled up the ladder of pegs hammered in the trunk, but felt Logan's apelike hand close around my ankle. I kicked down as hard as I could and heard a yelp of pain then a thud as he fell back on the grass. 'Why you little bugger!' he cried and came back after me, but by that time I was on to the platform, which was lurching all over the tree, shredding rotten planks on to Logan's ascending head. I leapt for the top of the wall, teetered there long enough to see Mayer running down the garden, then jumped into the street.

As I landed on the pavement some photostats escaped from the file, but seeing that Logan had failed to make the wall I took time to pick them up, then ran down the street to where Charlie was waiting in a taxi.

'Where to?' she asked.

'The *Maggot*.'

As the taxi pulled away she gave me a kiss and said, 'Harris, you're cool. Why don't you marry me?'

24 *Exeunt Omnes*

I spent the rest of that week-end with lawyers, new ones suggested by Gorton. With their help my case was postponed and three weeks later, after further police inquiries, dismissed.

On Sunday morning Mayer was found dead in his flat at Gray's Inn. Cause of death was diagnosed as barbiturate poisoning, the usual mixture of alcohol and sleeping pills. Did he mean to do it? That was hard to tell, since he didn't write a farewell note or speak to anyone after leaving the Bosanquet house. He left his whole estate – £218,000 – to a sister in Brighton.

The *Maggot* came out on the eve of the vote for the Labour Leadership. They had it all: the Dynatrax stock fraud, the attempt to frame me, the murder of Arbuthnot. Bosanquet withdrew his name from the ballot and later resigned his seat in the Commons.

The Irishman was never identified.

Arbuthnot's body was found in an abandoned mine shaft by

the Forestry Commission. His real name was Scarlatti. His mother had his ashes flown back to California and scattered on a lake near San Diego.

John Harvey, a director of Dynatrax, was charged with conspiracy to pervert the course of justice, but the case came unstuck. He and his chairman, Sir Godfrey Rawlinson, are now awaiting trial for fraud.

Logan was the only one to feel the rigour of the law. Convicted of being an accessory to Arbuthnot's murder, he also turned out to be involved in a drugs racket, which was how Mayer managed to set up events in Amsterdam so quickly. He got a total of fourteen years on both charges.

Bosanquet survived, as such men do. He was cleared of connivance in the fraud and protested ignorance of Mayer's activities. He has taken a job with the Planned Population Campaign at a nominal salary, which he can afford, the *Defendant* having paid him £60,000 for the serial rights of his memoirs. There is talk of a place on the Arts Council, and growing pressure for his return to Parliament.

The *Maggot*'s circulation almost doubled in the wake of the story, but is on the decline again. For a while I became a national celebrity, invited to take part in televised discussions and constantly recognized in pubs. But the fuss soon died down. Desmond changed his mind about the book on T.E.M.C. and is bringing it out in the spring (*Vandals of the Earth*, Galway Press, £2.80).

Charlie and I never got it together. A week before the wedding she left for Nepal and sent me a crate of champagne.

At the moment I'm staying with my aunt in Cornwall, working on a book about the K.G.B. I still don't have an agent.